HELL'S REVENGE

PRINCESS OF HELL #3

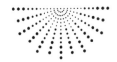

EVE LANGLAIS

CHAPTER ONE

*L*ucky me, I had the three most important men in my life sitting down for a nice family dinner. The irony of having Satan, my dear daddy, and the words 'nice' and 'family' used together did not escape me. After some careful negotiation, I'd made sure my father would behave at this and future dinners—we'd even signed the contract in blood. With my dad, you could never exercise too much caution.

But I didn't need his promise—with sub clauses in writing—for this particular meal. My father currently beamed like an escaped mental patient. Kind of freaky for the uninitiated, but as his daughter, I considered it endearing.

The reason for his joy? I'd just announced David was moving in with Auric and me.

"I can't believe it, my daughter living in sin with not one man but two. You do a father proud," he said, toasting the occasion. I swear he almost wiped a tear.

Auric rolled his eyes, familiar with my father's antics, but poor David appeared taken aback. My father's sense of humor took some getting used to.

Life since we'd vanquished the hooded one had returned to normal, or as normal as it could get for a princess of Hell. I'd avoided, in my usual head-in-the-sand fashion, some of the things Gabriel had told me when I captured him. My cowled nemesis, for the curious, was a fallen angel who'd delighted in torturing me. When I finally got him on his knees, subservient to the point of my sword, he began to spout all kinds of crap. I'd decapitated the freaky bastard rather than listen to his monologue. Like hello, I'd seen enough movies to know letting the enemy talk gave them time to wait for reinforcements. Besides, I had more important things that required my attention such as an aroused libido that wasn't in the mood to exercise patience.

Apart from Gabriel, who I refused to discuss, Auric kept trying to talk to me about my absent mother. As if I wanted to think about the bitch who'd abandoned me with a curse on my mind—not! Sticking my fingers in my ears and humming soon brought those attempted conversations to a halt. Poor Auric, I was really making him practice his sighs of impatience a lot lately.

In a nutshell, I refused to dwell on the crap I'd gone through lately, and in an attempt for a life of normalcy, I'd arranged for my dad to come for a nice family dinner—cooked by Auric, of course. Anything less would have seen me punished for cruelty.

The pasta primavera came out divine, the chicken succulent, the conversation ribald; in other words, dinner appeared a complete success.

It figured my aunt Fate would fuck with it. A knock sounded at the door, and I'd like to say I heard haunting music, that my eyes rolled back and I experienced an ominous premonition. Alas, my precognitive skills were limited to the knot that formed in my stomach. I knew from a lifetime of experience that if things were going well something would come along to screw with me, which meant whoever stood on the other side of that steel-reinforced barrier was about to fuck up the nice new life I'd settled into.

"Don't answer," I said in a childish attempt to avoid whatever calamity waited for me in the hallway.

Apparently, my worry was contagious because Auric grabbed his holy sword before he headed to the door when a second knock sounded. Auric twisted the knob and swung the door open, keeping care to ensure his bulky body remained in front of the doorway, blocking direct access inside. It also meant I couldn't see who'd come calling.

I drummed my fingers on the table as David stood and moved to stand in front of me protectively. My men, throwbacks to a time of chivalry when women were fainting damsels. Cute and yet so unnecessary. They knew by now, even if they refused to acknowledge it, I could take care of myself.

I heard a chair sliding back and hitting the floor. Looking over, I saw my father staring at the door, a look of stunned surprise on his face. The knot in my stomach tightened into a really painful ball. I'd never seen my dad look so spooked, and if the caller had the ability to freak out Lucifer, Lord of Hell, it didn't bode well for me.

"No, it can't be," he muttered.

A burning need rose in me, overcoming my trepidation. I had to see what had my father looking as if he'd seen a ghost. I walked around David, who, to my surprise, didn't try and stop me.

"Hello, Lucifer." A petite woman, with creamy smooth skin I envied, walked in. "It's been a long time." Dressed in a green suit that would have looked appropriate in the boardroom, she didn't sport claws, or horns, heck, she didn't even have a weapon.

The innocuous appearance didn't matter though; panic engulfed me. Taking a step back, I bumped against the dinner table. I didn't understand my reaction. My instincts screamed danger, even as my men stood there, letting the stranger into my home. The dinner knife I palmed was hidden behind my back.

"Do you know this woman, Dad?" I asked. Did Auric know her as well? Was that why he'd let her in?

"Yes, and so do you," my father replied, the expression on his face drawn, his eyes full of sorrow.

I hated cryptic answers. They made my head hurt. The woman, with long hair and a familiar face, looked at me. The room spun, and I swooned. Thankfully, there were several pairs of hands there to catch me.

I regained consciousness seated on Auric's lap with David handing me a glass of water, which I took with shaking hands. Despite my fainting spell, the center stage currently belonged to the woman watching me enigmatically, my long-lost mother.

"What's your name?" I suddenly felt a monstrous need to know. I had no memories of this stranger, the woman who had birthed me and abandoned me. By some kind of freaky magic or curse, no one had recalled her, but now that I had a face, I wanted an identity to go with it. A name I could curse. What? In my twenties and she finally decided to show up? Fuck her. I wasn't about to make this easy for her.

She arched a brow, and I found her smile condescending. "I would have thought your first question would have been why I am here."

No, my first question was actually 'Do you want to die agonizingly or...well, really agonizingly?' In my world, revenge wasn't just approved of by my father; it was expected.

However, killing her meant not getting some answers, and despite my intense hatred, I found myself curious. "Fine then, why are you here?" I let my impatience show. I hated momentous news before dessert. Especially since I knew Auric had spent the afternoon crafting a caramel-topped cheesecake from scratch. Long-lost mother who abandoned me versus decadent cheesecake dripping in creamy caramel delight? I wondered how quickly I could get rid of her. Of course, her next words pretty much blew all thoughts of dessert out of my mind.

"Why to witness the birth of your child. My

grandchild. Which reminds me, congratulations to the fathers."

Now, there were a myriad of ways a person could comport themselves when meeting their mother for the first time. They could fall on their long-lost parent, crying and hugging while trying to blubber how happy they were to be reunited. Gag me with a spoon but I hated sappy shit like that.

A girl could coldly tell the absentee mother to shove her attempt at reconciliation where the sun never shone. Rude snark was a touch better.

A person could even faint in a damsel-like fashion or run from the room screaming, "I hate you" just before they slammed a door shut.

But, as a princess of Hell, I tended to lean toward the more dramatic—I did have a reputation to uphold after all. I threw a knife at my visiting mother's head.

In my defense, it was only a butter knife—unfortunately—and I knew, even before I fired it with deadly intent, it would never make its target—an even bigger shame.

Gasp in shock all you wanted, the woman had not only abandoned me as a young child she'd also left a nasty spell on my mind that made me writhe in pain if I so much as said the word 'mother'. To say I had anger issues was putting it mildly.

Her teensy-tiny announcement of my pregnancy by not one but two of my lovers? That was just the icing on the cake. Not that I believed her claim, of course. I mean, seriously, me pregnant?

Anyway, possible uterine situations aside, I chucked a butter knife at her. It hit an invisible wall and went clattering noisily to the floor.

Chaos erupted, most of it caused by me, and I found myself manhandled, without the usual erotic groping, until I stood hidden by the broad back of my consort, Auric, while David, my second lover, grabbed me in a wrestler hold from behind—again, a lot more fun when we were all naked.

"Let me go," I growled as I thrashed in David's implacable grip.

"Not until you calm down," he retorted.

My mature reply was to slam my foot down on his instep. A human would have dropped me, screaming like a stuck pig. However, my lovers weren't one hundred percent human, so David didn't even grunt. Instead, the jerk just lifted me high enough that my flailing feet pedaled in midair.

Frustrated and still in the mood to inflict some bodily harm, I appealed to my other lover. "Auric, you tell him to unhand me this instant." I disliked that my request came out sounding petulant, although it probably went well with my jutting lower lip.

Vivid green eyes met mine as Auric turned to peer back at me. "He'll let you go when you can comport yourself as a lady."

I snorted. Like that would ever happen. "When Hell freezes over." At his arched brow, I flushed and amended my statement, "Again."

See, not so long ago, the pit of damnation had experienced its very first winter. I'd really enjoyed the pure white look, but as it turned out, Hell freezing over was a bad thing for humanity. Who'd have guessed there was some secret force out there keeping track of all the vows made with conditions such as 'I'll sleep with you when Hell freezes over'. Needless to say, when Hades' temperature plummeted, a lot of women found themselves putting out whether they wanted to or not.

I snapped my wandering mind back to the situation at hand instead of a past I'd conquered.

"She's got a right to her anger," said my father.

I beamed at my dad. Sue me. I took pride in being a daddy's girl. But be warned, if you decided to sue, my dad had the best lawyers working for him in Hell.

"Thank you, Daddy," I simpered with a flutter of

my lashes that made him snort. "I've got all kinds of reasons to be pissed, so let me at the cow."

My men ignored me and when I looked sideways at my father, waiting for him to come to my aide again, he shrugged helplessly.

"Some Satan you are," I grumbled.

Actually, if I weren't concerned with possibly hurting the people I loved most in the world—my dad and my lovers—I could have broken free using my innate magic. Their wellbeing in the face of my still not entirely reliable power and a twisted set of rules and morals, which I'd created for myself, made me stay my magical hand. Besides, a girly part of me enjoyed the manhandling. It made me think of our bedroom games, where one would hold me down while the other did superhot things to my body.

However, I was allowing myself to get distracted again, pleasant as the mental images were. I brought my naughty mind back to the present in time to hear my father speak.

"Actually, your men might have the right idea. I'd like to hear what the woman has to say before you rip her head off."

"Well, I don't want to hear," I muttered stubbornly as I struggled anew to free myself. I was sure my mother had plenty of handy excuses as to why she'd abandoned me, and I wasn't interested in any of them. The only thing that would satisfy me involved wiping the smug look off her face. But all the invectives in the world wouldn't loosen David's grip. Damned shapeshifter, he just had to be as strong as he was good looking. What a jerk.

Rescue came from an unlikely source. "Oh, let her go. She can't hurt me." The petite form of my X chromosome donator came into view as my mother walked around Auric.

If I hadn't been so pissed, I would have laughed at the look on my father's face as she brushed him in passing—part shock, part lust, and a touch of fear, not a reassuring sign. Not much shook my dad, but this tiny woman sure did. I disliked her even more because of it.

"You've got a lot of fucking nerve coming back," I spat, even as David's arms tightened instead of loosening.

A chair scraped as someone dragged it across the floor. A moment later, I found myself handed from one Neanderthal to another as David passed me over to Auric, who sat me on his lap. An admittedly more comfortable position without the manacling arms, but one I already knew I wouldn't escape until I either calmed down or my mother left. I didn't like either option, so I settled on sneaky and waited for an opening.

"There's no need to be so hostile." My mother's condescending tone did little to ease my irritation.

"Actually, Muriel has every right to be upset." Auric came to my rescue and earned himself a blowjob for later, my newfound specialty. "You abandoned her as a small child without an explanation or further contact and now come waltzing back into her life as if nothing's wrong, only to drop a bomb. I think she's entitled to her anger."

My mother made a moue of annoyance, and her green eyes flashed with ire. "So why not let her kill me if you think I'm so evil?"

"I'm tempted to, but Lucifer's right. We need answers, but don't worry." Auric's voice dropped, and when he next spoke, I shivered in delight at his deadly tone. "If I don't like the answers, or you try to hurt Muriel again, I will kill you myself."

Ooh, a blowjob and more. I did so love Auric. I should have known he'd take my side. And damn, did I find it hot when he got all protective and dangerous.

"And you, kitty, are you also going to kill me?" My mother turned eyes meant to look innocent on my other lover—David, my giant, blond, shapeshifting panther.

I almost snorted again. Was I the only one who could read the deceit behind her calculated gaze?

"Muriel's wellbeing is my main concern. Hurt her and I'll have to hurt you." David spoke nonchalantly as his hand came to rest on my shoulder. I tilted my head sideways and rubbed my cheek against it. Make that two blowjobs for later.

My mother's lips pursed, and her eyes narrowed. "I don't have time for these childish games. There are grave matters afoot."

"When aren't there?" I muttered. It seemed lately, along with the usual assassination attempts that came with my position as a princess of Hell, life hadn't stopped throwing curve balls at me. I already knew shit was coming, and I'd invested in a new wardrobe of black to handle the stains—really hot and slutty leather outfits with easy access for the celebratory sex that usually occurred after I'd prevailed.

Given that my life consistently insisted on being complicated, I no longer bothered to worry about it. I'd handle it if, and when, it arrived. I didn't lack confidence, and I'd earned my right to boast. Heck, I'd almost single-handedly saved Hades from a rebellion not long after I met Auric. Then, when a massive spell turned the pit I'd grown up in into a winter wonderland, I killed Gabriel, the freaky, spell-casting angel gone mad. And to top it all off, with the help of my super fun nympho magic and two energetic lovers, I relit the flames of Hell. Whatever load of crap fate had in store for me, I figured I could handle it. In my world, it was all about attitude.

"The baby you carry—"

I cut her off. "Listen, lady. I don't know what makes you think I'm pregnant, but I assure you, I'm not. I mean, don't you think I would have noticed?" I waited for Auric to second my statement, but instead, silence reigned. An icy finger tickled its way down my spine. "Um, Auric, tell her I can't be pregnant."

"I wish I could, but there's something different about you lately." Auric spoke quietly, and I shifted in his lap to peer into his face. I didn't like what I saw in his eyes.

In a panic, I looked at my father, who shrugged helplessly, and then to David, who wouldn't meet my eyes. "No. Un-uh. I'd know if I had a bun in the oven." I tried to count in my head the date of my last period and came up blank. Not a good sign because even I knew my math wasn't that bad. Cold dread gripped me as the truth tried to batter through my denial. Sure, I'd thought of motherhood—way, way in the future, once my life settled down. But pregnant now, and as impossible as it seemed, by two men as my mother claimed? I refused to take just her word for it. However, until I could talk to someone I trusted to give me the unvarnished truth, I needed some more answers. Starting with, what the fuck was my mother?

"Who and what are you?"

I swear we could have heard a cockroach fart the room got so quiet. Apparently, I wasn't the only one suffering from that particular curiosity.

"I am Gaia."

"I didn't ask for your sexual orientation. I asked for your name."

My mother's brow creased, and Auric's chest shook as he rumbled with laughter.

I scowled. "What? You know I hate it when I don't get the joke."

"I am Gaia," my mother repeated, enunciating each letter clearly. "Also known as Mother Earth."

Heat rose in my cheeks at my mistake, but I wouldn't let my embarrassing error over her name stop me from speaking my mind. "Anyone ever tell you that you suck at the mother part?"

15

For a moment, I thought I'd gone too far, as Gaia —I refused to call her mother now that I had a name for her—puffed out her chest and her hair lifted as if by an invisible breeze. Even unschooled as I was in magic, I recognized the fact that she'd drawn power around herself.

I'd never know what she meant to do with it though—maybe wash my mouth out with some esoteric soap—because my dad finally yanked his balls out of hiding and used them.

"Enough." Dad said the word quietly, but the threat in his tone rang clear. To everyone's surprise, Gaia backed down, the magic in her deflating like a balloon with a tiny hole.

I almost stuck my tongue out in a childish gesture of triumph, but restrained myself. Look at me, growing up and acting like an adult. Not!

Before I could cause more trouble, Auric spoke. "Why have you returned?"

"I need the child she carries."

Gaia's statement, boldly spoken, shocked everyone into stillness, and my chance arrived. I sprang, lightning quick, from Auric's lap and slammed into the bitch's smaller form. We both hit the floor, hard, and I managed to wrap my hands around her neck and bang her head on the floor a few times before someone yanked me off her. It didn't stop my mouth from running though.

"You sick bitch! You keep your hands off the baby I'm not pregnant with. You'll get nothing from me. I wouldn't even piss in your mouth if you were on fire, you...you..."

I would have said a lot more, some of it pretty inventive and involving household items she could shove in her various orifices, but I found my mouth plastered by Auric's, and as usual when he kissed me, I forgot what was going on around me.

My magic stirred as his lips slanted over mine. An easily roused beast, my nympho powers never missed a chance to draw in sexual energy. At the back of my mind, I recognized Auric's attempt at distraction, but I allowed it. I was done talking with Gaia for the moment, and the sooner she left, the quicker my boys would give me some breathing room —and a good fuck. Then I'd go hunting for answers of my own.

First though, I'd take the opportunity presented to recharge my batteries and have fun whilst doing so. I vaguely heard the sounds of people leaving, and when familiar hands, four of them to be exact, began divesting me of my clothing, I knew my dad and the woman who'd incubated me had left.

I'm sure some people would have some choice names for me, given I openly flaunted the fact I had not one but two lovers. Call me a slut or a whore all you want, you jealous bitches. I loved my unusual threesome lifestyle, for while Auric was my soulmate and consort, I also deeply loved David. The two of them in my bed and heart made me ecstatically happy, and I enjoyed some truly kick-ass magic as an added benefit.

Not to mention the orgasms were out of this world.

Of course, pleasure sometimes came with pain. Naked, wet, and horny, I couldn't wait to get sucked or fucked. Instead, I ended up splayed on my stomach over David's naked lap.

"Aw, come on," I complained—not too hard, though. I did enjoy some firm correction from time to time. But like it or not, I still played the part of unwilling submissive. "She totally deserved that for interrupting our nice family dinner." I tried to rear up, a foolhardy attempt what with David's large hand holding me firmly down.

The first crack on my ass stung, but I didn't cry out. Tough was one of my middle names.

"That's for acting like a spoiled brat," Auric announced. Another sharp smack followed, a much harder one, and I bit my lip. My consort had learned I could handle a lot and no longer held back as much when he punished me. "That was for acting before thinking." A flurry of slaps peppered my bottom, alternating between my cheeks. The pinching pain made me gasp, but the more he heated the skin of my buttocks with his hands, the more my desire coiled, ready to spring.

"And that," he said, his voice husky, "is for tempting the bitch to hurt you and not listening to me." The force behind his blows lightened, and I smiled, unseen, as I knew what would happen next.

I usually misbehaved for a reason, and when Auric's hand slipped between my thighs to stroke my slick flesh, I moaned. Pleasure and pain, say what you would, they went hand in hand—or should I say prick in pussy?

His calloused fingers gripped my burning cheeks, and I hissed, crying out as he used my spread position to rub the swollen head of his rod against my clit. The direct stimulation made me squirm and gasp. He teased me with his shaft, slapping it against my cleft and then sliding it back and forth against me.

"Give it to me," I begged.

"Tell me you're going to be a good girl," he replied.

"Never." I wouldn't make a promise I couldn't keep.

"What am I going to do with you?" Auric growled. He rewarded my defiant stance with more slaps to my pussy and clit with his cock. I moaned, the zinging pleasure of his punishment making me hot and wet for him.

"Fuck me. Fuck me hard."

Auric's fingers dug into my cheeks, and he sheathed his cock in my throbbing sex. I yelled, the instant filling of my channel by his wide shaft making my channel clench around him. He moved inside me, in and out. He started slow, his balls lightly tapping my clit. He did that just to tease me. He knew I liked it hard and fast, and as I continued to squeeze my pussy around him, tighter than OJ's glove, he increased his pace until he slammed in and out of me so hard his balls slapped my nub, making me keen.

Against my tummy, I could feel David's excitement as he watched Auric take his turn pumping my sex. My big kitty had voyeuristic tendencies, and I freely admitted I found having him as an audience titillating.

I struggled to shift position with a moaned, "I want to suck you." Those magic words saw David release me, and with a little shuffling, I repositioned myself. Instead of being draped over his lap, I faced David, on my knees. My face ended up poised just above his groin and a cock that tempted me.

I slid my lips over his engorged head, inching him slowly in, teasing him. Auric resumed pumping me from behind and shoved a heavy hand in the middle of my back, forcing me down onto David's dick. I loved it when he got all dominant. I braced my hands on David's thighs and then, with the ease of recent practice, bobbed my head up and down David's prick while slamming my ass back against Auric's groin, driving his cock to the hilt in my channel.

Hot, fast, and sweaty. That was how I wanted my sex, and they gave it to me. When Auric started lightly slapping my already sensitized bottom, my pussy clenched and then exploded. Lost in the throes of my orgasm, I vaguely noticed David had grabbed my hair to hold my head in the right position for him to mouth fuck me. And then, like a synchronized sex team, my lovers came in a rush of cream and sexual power that filled me up in more ways than one.

They released me, and I stood up. I stretched

with a smile to put the Cheshire Cat to shame. My magical reservoir was filled to overflowing, but that didn't prevent me from crooking a finger at them from the bathroom door. Warmed up and still in the mood, I planned to make use of the large shower stall we'd had installed.

And might I say round two ended up just as much fun?

CHAPTER TWO

*P*art of my devious plan to avoid a talk meant tiring my men out. Not that hard considering marathon sex tended to have a sleepy effect. I knew I couldn't avoid some of the revelations unearthed today forever, but before everyone started telling me what they wanted me to do, I wanted to be forewarned and informed so I could make my own decisions.

No one told me what to do, but they would try.

Auric's plan would involve sitting down with my mother and talking in a grown-up manner, and that just wasn't my style. People often thought and accused me of acting without thinking. How untrue. I thought about a lot of stuff and then ignored the right thing to do in favor of doing what my gut and impatient nature demanded.

First on the agenda—finding out what might be growing in my tummy. I found the idea of pregnancy by both my lovers, whom I'd only begun dual bedding a few weeks ago, a little unlikely. Unless they possessed super sperm. Memories of the swallowing blowjobs I gave them made me wince as I imagined their swimmers coasting through my digestive system in red capes. At times, having an imagination proved a real curse.

Having watched my fair share of alien and paranormal movies, Auric's comment that he sensed something different about me kind of freaked me out. Like Rosemary, did I have some kind of monster growing in my tummy? Of course, in Rosemary's case, it just turned out to be a false antichrist. Given my mixed parentage of Earth and Hell, along with the DNA of my fallen angel and kitty cat, my baby, even if I was pregnant, would put Heinz 57 to shame.

All of my musings, though, hinged on the possibility of a bun in my oven. It occurred to me to run to the pharmacy and get one of those little sticks to pee on. But really, that seemed too simple, and could I count on a human pregnancy test working on a supernatural baby? Not to mention, I really didn't want to pee on my hand. I'd never had good aim and insisted on actual bathrooms on road trips, having peed on my own feet on the side of the road one time too many.

I had a better plan to see if some fertilization had occurred, a plan more my style.

Sneaking out of bed was not as easy as it sounded considering I slept between two large male bodies. Scooting out involved a lot of touching—okay, I'll admit to a little stroking. Who could resist all that yummy male flesh? When Auric opened a sleepy eye to peer at me as I slid off him, I mouthed, "I gotta go pee."

It wasn't a complete lie. I did have to pee, but I also had another goal in mind, one I intended to accomplish alone. I used the toilet and quickly brushed my teeth and hair. Not having time for a shower, I settled for a quick wipe down of my sticky body and a spray of perfume. Where I was going I'd still probably end up the cleanest and prettiest smelling thing, shower or not.

The bifold doors to the laundry center squeaked, and I winced. No avenging angel came barreling through the bathroom door. A shame. Auric truly was a sight to see when he got riled.

I quickly pulled from the dryer a clean pair of undies, jeans, and a top. I didn't find a bra, but I didn't worry about it. While a little heavy, my breasts still hung perkily. Although...I cupped them and bit my lip as I noted they not only felt larger but also had a tenderness to them that I'd attributed to the energetic lovemaking of my men. But swollen boobs didn't mean anything.

How about the fact I've gotten chubby? I silently cursed when I went to button my jeans and had to suck in my tummy to do so. Damned dryer must have shrunk them. That was the only explanation. I'd inherited my father's stubborn gene though, so even in the face of growing evidence, I still remained skeptical about my supposed pregnancy. Heck, given the way Auric cooked for me, weight gain wasn't entirely impossible.

Dressed, I ran into a shoes dilemma and settled for some flip-flops I found in my gym bag. I used them for the communal showers at my gym, even though my very nature prevented me from catching yucky foot diseases. Walking barefoot was something I did in the comfort of my home or on a hot sandy beach, not in public places.

Ready, if oddly attired, I noted I'd wasted enough time. If I didn't get moving, Auric was sure to come looking for me. He knew my penchant for plots with little planning. For once though, what I intended wasn't actually dangerous. Well, not to me anyways. Anyone who got in my way...that was a whole other matter.

Drawing on the magical power brimming in me after all the glorious sex, I opened a portal to Hell. The familiar scent of home, brimstone, and dry heat filled the bathroom. I stepped toward the doorway between Earth and Hades just as the bathroom door crashed open.

"Muriel!" Auric growled, not sounding at all happy with me.

I gave a quick wave at my naked and totally pissed looking consort before diving through the portal. As soon as my feet hit the ground on the other side, I cut my link to the portal to shut it, but not before I heard Auric bellow, "I'm going to tan your ass when I get my hands on you!"

Naughty man. I almost turned right around to take him up on his titillating threat. I did so love his version of punishment, just ask my creaming pussy, but I had a task to accomplish and little time to complete it because Auric could follow me to Hell by calling a doorway of his own. First, though, he'd need to figure out where I'd gone. The nine circles of Hell were a sprawling expanse that even ancient demonic cartographers had yet to fully map.

Confident I'd have plenty of time to get my questions answered, I strode down the cluttered streets of the third circle in the pit, the sprawling tenement housing of the damned looming all around. Contrary to popular belief, Hades wasn't all about punishing people for eternity—not like the old days, as my father liked to reminisce. Actually, most damned who ended up in the pit paid their dues rather quickly.

Told a white lie in your living life like fibbing about the existence of Santa to your kids? You served as a waiter in a family restaurant for each year you upheld that foolish belief. Didn't sound too bad until a person realized demonic children took misbehaving to a whole new level.

Cheated on your faithful wife? You found yourself a magically-induced eunuch working in a brothel, a day for every time you'd banged your mistress.

My father had fine-tuned his punishments over the years to fit the crime. Gone were the days of people being stretched on racks with their entrails ripped out over and over for centuries. Now, we had tome upon tome detailing the various punishments every single act of evil earned, most resulting in menial tasks that kept the machine that was Hell turning. Although, every now and then, for old time's sake, my dad would go medieval on someone's ass. But in his defense, it was all about PR. He paid careful attention to the polls, and if he found the damned in his kingdom complaining he was going soft, he quickly disabused them of that notion.

What about Heaven, you might ask? From what I'd heard, if you managed to actually pass their super strict entrance test, you ended up spending eternity bored out of your mind. Given the choice between them, I knew what I'd choose. Variety was the spice of life.

Before you began thinking Hell was a nice place to live, keep in mind that those who'd truly embraced evil while alive got punished in extremely inventive ways. The warlord who executed whole villages, including the children? Let's just say his screams on the hour, every hour, resonated through the nine circles of Hell, our version of a cuckoo clock. And you definitely didn't want to know what my father liked to do to rapists, even as I, and women everywhere, applauded him on his tough stance. Men, on the other hand, tended to blanch, wince, and cover their cocks.

Yes, Hades could be an interesting place for those who'd done their time, or for someone like me who happened to share a familial relation with the big man, it was a familiar haven to visit and enjoy adulation. I'd spent most of my formative years in the pit, and even though I now lived on the mortal plane, I enjoyed coming home, even if my clothes ended up a total write-off. Brimstone just wasn't a smell that came out easily.

My mind rambled in odd directions as I tried not to think too hard of Auric's reaction when he got to Hell and didn't find me. He probably expected me to go to my father's palace in search of answers, a logical assumption. However, the person—er, creature—I needed to speak to had taken some time off to recharge her batteries.

A shrivelled prune of a female, the mage I currently planned to visit, enjoyed the same type of nympho magic as I did. Sick as she made me when she talked about the things she did with her lovers, I couldn't deny she was a fount of knowledge and, even more astonishing, honest. An oxymoronic state when you considered where she resided, but she'd helped me before, first in dispelling the spell of fear placed on my mind and a few times since when I'd contacted her with questions about my magic.

As I strutted the length of the dusty road that led to her home—her 'pleasure den' she'd cackled when giving me the directions—the milling damned cleared a path for me. Recognition shone in their eyes. Adulation surely imbued their whispers of, "It's the princess."

Knowing I'd just brightened their day with my presence, I waved and smiled in thanks. Just because I didn't visit often anymore didn't mean I'd lost my ability to awe those who lived in my father's domain. After a while, though, I realized while the damned kept moving out of my way, they didn't seem to be looking at me when they did it. As a matter of fact, their pleasure at seeing me now seemed clouded with fear—and excitement.

Suspicious, I stopped and turned around and suddenly wished I hadn't ditched my boyfriends.

In Hell, only the toughest survive, and I freely admitted I was one tough-ass bitch. However, even I had limits to what I could accomplish, and seeing the bully gang of demons coming toward me with evil intent in their eyes, I sighed.

Dammit, I'd just had my nails done.

I counted more than a dozen demons, lower caste squat beasts, but still dangerous. Their evident stalking surprised me. One, they had to know who I was, the most awesome princess Hell had ever had, and even if they didn't recognize my estimable person, everyone knew that my dad didn't look kindly on his flock of souls being abused. However, knowing my dad would rip their heads off their bodies and shove them up their asses provided little consolation as they moved to circle around me.

I looked around for someone I could send to fetch the guards—yes, even Hell was policed—but the souls who'd thronged the street had vanished, gone to hide until the dust settled.

Not one to scamper before adversity, I decided to try intimidation first because reasoning with thugs, in my mind, was for cowards. "Back off, dirt bags! You really don't want to mess with me."

The tallest demon in the bunch took a step forward, his ugly countenance rendered even more puke-worthy by the fact that his nose appeared sheared from his face. "Did someone come trolling without her consort or father?" He cracked his knuckles. "What a stupid little princess."

Okay, so they did recognize me and weren't intimidated. Maybe it was time I also hired my dad's PR firm. My reputation deserved better than this blatant disrespect. "I never said I was scared. I was trying to show concern over your future wellbeing. In case you hadn't heard, I can take care of myself just fine."

The noose of bodies around me drew closer, and I wished I'd thought to bring along some of my silver daggers for what should have been a quick in-and-out information-gathering mission. Complacency was ever my enemy. Even bare-handed though, I'd acquit myself well and fight like the most rabid of hellhounds.

Thinking of the dogs I'd grown up with made me wish I'd adopted a pup out of the last litter; however, as Auric reminded me, hellhounds would draw attention on the mortal plane. Their red, glowing eyes tended to freak out the humans. My poor misunderstood babies.

As usual, in times of stress, my mind had wandered, but it snapped back quickly when the leader said, "Azazel sends his regards."

"Not that fucker again," I snarled. It figured my scorned demonic suitor would have a claw behind this. Even though I'd beaten Azazel's ass and my dad had hauled him off for punishment, apparently he still seemed determined to cause havoc in my life. See, this was what happened when you let the bad guys live. And people wondered why I enjoyed decapitation so much. Very few enemies rose from that final method.

As for Azazel, I'd rectify that problem myself

when I finished here. Screw punishment and fuck listening to their screams as you tortured them. Kill them. I had little patience for those who crossed me, unlike my father, who liked to hear their pleas for forgiveness.

The air behind me stirred as the first cowardly thug thought to take me unawares. Fool. I never took my eyes from the leader in front of me as I kicked backwards, only belatedly remembering I had worn my flip-flops instead of my favored stilettos. I'd put enough force in the strike, though, that I earned a grunt. But like the matador swinging the red cape, my counterattack spurred the others on.

In the movies, fight scenes were a chaotic mess of events with lots of noise, awesome music, and cool Matrix-like moves. In real life, fist fighting was sweaty, painful on the knuckles, bloody, and tiring. I ducked, punched, kicked, tripped, and gave myself a workout to rival the evil Pilates one I had on tape at home. Killing demons bare-handed was hard, given I couldn't rip their hearts out; my acrylic nails just weren't made for that type of abuse. I had to settle for breaking their necks.

And the bastards weren't cooperating! Not to mention, they were overwhelming me with sheer numbers.

My magic, fickle at times, reacted to the threat to my life and filled me with a rush. The guttural words to banish the demons came to my tongue, words in a language I neither spoke nor understood. Not that I cared. I was familiar with the result and spoke them without hesitation.

With an almost audible whoosh, magic rushed from me in a tidal wave that engulfed my assailants. I staggered under the pressure of using so much power all at once, but my reward was to see the demons explode in a cloud of sifting ash, which coated my skin in a grimy layer. If I hadn't needed a shower before, I sure as heck did now.

A smaller demon watching on the outskirts, which my magic missed, brave when amidst the ranks of the bigger demons, turned tail and ran when he saw his compatriots reduced to dust. I would have shaken my fist after him and called him some rude names, but, instead, I groaned as a portal opened several yards down the street. Out poured a dozen fresh demons, their murderous intent all too clear.

With my magic sucked dry and fatigue pulling at me, I did the only thing I could. I turned tail and ran. I really hated it when I resorted to stupidity; after all, I'd also seen the movies where the heroine tried to outrun the bad guys. One of two things usually happened. The hero jumped out of nowhere to save her—*Um, hello, Auric, where are you?*—or the bad guys got the girl. I pumped my legs faster.

My bad luck got even worse as a new threat dropped down from the sky like some dark, and yet stupidly sexy, vulture. The human-looking newcomer stood square in my path, and given his stature—think titan—and his width—like a freaking wall—I skidded to a stop. Caught between two hard places and neither of them naked or part of my ménage, I prayed—to my dad, of course—for help.

The dark stranger, standing there dressed in black from head to toe, somehow managed to convey more menace than the rampaging demons coming up behind me. He smiled at me—*hot damn, he's hot*—flashing a pointed set of fangs.

A vampire! Rarer than modern media portrayed, they were what happened to a mortal when he sold his soul to the devil. Shocking, I know. I'd read all the Anne Rice books, only to discover the whole drink-my-blood-and-live-forever shtick was false. Although, the fact that they liked to drink blood proved totally true and, yes, gross, which I knew from experience. I'd tried it once when I bit some wizard who wouldn't take no for an answer. Needless to say, he didn't like my permanent hickey and backed off.

But back to Tall, Dark, and Probably going to eat me. I'd always wanted to meet a real vampire, but unfortunately, most tended to die rather quickly after turning. Apparently, when they said 'no daylight', they were really freaking serious. Even the slightest UV ray filtered through a dark, cloudy day was enough to melt them right out of existence.

My knowledge of vampires, though, and the lack of a wooden stake—Brazilian rosewood being the most effective—didn't help me at all when faced with one who stared at me with dark, enigmatic eyes and a dimple in one cheek.

I cursed at the fact that, even given my danger, my damned nympho magic perked up at his masculine grin. Somehow, the fact I that found him attractive, even as I knew he was going to attempt to kill me, seemed wrong.

I bet he's got a hard stake, my snide magic murmured in my mind with a lusty chuckle. Some people had an angel on one shoulder and a devil on the other as the voices of their conscience. Me, I had a whole legion of little devils, and while entertaining, they really made me question my sanity at times.

"Stand behind me." His voice, low and resonant, wrapped around me and brought forth an involuntary shiver, the kind that moistened a pussy and tightened nipples.

"What did you say?" Confused not only by his words but my body's reaction, I could only gape at him dazedly. A moment of inattention that almost cost me my life. I barely managed to duck the swinging demonic claws aimed at my head.

Strong hands grabbed me, and in a move Auric would have probably applauded, I found myself kneeling in the dirt behind the vampire. It seemed I'd gotten my wish for help, even if the packaging wasn't what I'd expected. I struggled to my feet, not that I needed to worry about any demons getting past the battle machine in front of me.

The vampire moved with a fluid grace and boneless agility that made me want to fan myself. Seriously, he oozed freaking hot. And he was fast, superhero fast. One by one, he dispatched the demons using a pair of onyx daggers in his hands that gleamed as darkly as his eyes. He must have caught me watching because, as he took down my attackers in spinning moves I thought existed only in the video game *Tekken*, a grin spread across his face and his moves became even more flamboyant.

I turned away from him in an attempt to curb my way too interested libido in time to see a demon dart out from between a pair of ramshackle buildings. I yanked on the last dregs of my energy and, looking like a sluggish snail, I'm sure, kicked it in the groin. When the beast doubled over in pain—demons had such sensitive balls—I grabbed its head and dropped to the ground in a wrestler move that, with a little wrench, snapped its neck.

Auric liked to joke that I should wrestle for the WWE, but I'd seen too much hair pulling on that soap opera for me to risk my long locks.

I peered about wildly as I knelt on the ground, panting. I didn't see any more demons attempting to sneak up on me and a good thing, too, because I was completely drained, both physically and magically. I would remain weak and useless until I got home to recharge—a.k.a. until I enjoyed a naked tussle with my two men. Blame my hungry nympho power for what happened next.

The stranger, the stupidly sexy-looking dead dude, strode over to me. Nonchalance practically oozed from him as he stepped over the demon carcasses he'd dispatched. The bodies littered the ground in a gory mess. Only my magic or a death inflicted on the mortal plane ever made them evaporate into oily ash. When given a regular death in Hell, they decayed like any other corpse, unless fed to carrion feeders or hellhounds. Surprisingly enough, we had a decent recycling program in the pit, probably on account it wasn't easy smuggling things from the mortal side.

As I watched the vampire approach, I finally understood that expression 'a stupid deer caught in headlights'. I didn't move; I couldn't. For some reason I remained frozen in place, foolishly not fleeing, even if I still had a slim chance to escape. More annoyingly, I didn't want to run. My magic—that hungry parasite—wanted to see what would happen next. What did this stranger want from me? I almost held my breath in anticipation.

The vampire picked me up and held me close, close enough that I could feel something hard poking at me. "Is that an erection in your pocket, or are you wearing a cup?"

While vanity insisted he was overcome by my awesome good looks, assumptions could make a girl look stupid. It wasn't an attractive look, so I tried to avoid it.

"Touch it and find out," he teased.

Had he seriously dared me? If only I weren't involved with two other men, I would have totally groped him to find out. Okay, so I did make a grab, in the interest of knowing if I should avoid kneeing him in the balls. See, nothing wrong with information gathering.

It wasn't a cup. It was one hundred percent male erection, and it appeared his body wasn't the only big thing about him. Not that I cared, of course. I was happily involved with two men after all. Damn, I'm getting better at this whole lying to myself thing. I betcha Dad was wiping a tear in pride.

The vampire's arctic eyes, now hued the dark blue of a storm-tossed sea, peered down into mine. I stared right back and thus got an up-close glimpse when his orbs dilated to pure black. Probably not a good sign, and had I mentioned he looked hungry?

I'll bet princess blood is tasty. I knew my pussy certainly was according to my guys. Was it any wonder this vampire wanted a bite.

The stranger inhaled deeply, and I wanted to wince, wondering how I smelled considering everything that had happened since my last shower.

"What are you?" he asked in a thick voice while still staring at me with those freaky, iris-less eyes.

His ignorance surprised me. I'd assumed he'd come to my aid because of who I was. So I lied. Look at me following in my family's dishonest footsteps. "Me? Oh, I'm a mix of this and that," I replied, hedging. I'd learned in the past that relaying my parentage never ended up a good idea. The whole kill-the-daughter-of-Satan thing could really put a damper on things.

"Whatever you are, you smell delicious," he murmured before his lips found mine.

Now, the proper thing to do, considering my involvement in a committed relationship with two men, would have been to push him away and then kick his ass for taking liberties with me.

But I had nothing left to fight with, and my damned nympho magic appeared in no mood to pay attention to my morals. Oh no, instead my sex-based power clamped my lips tight to his. A cool esoteric breeze, the distinct flavor of his sexual energy, flowed into me.

I am ashamed to admit I shivered in delight. Where David projected animalistic heat and Auric bathed me in pure light, this man reminded me of cold darkness, and he fed a part of my magic I hadn't known existed, until now.

As a trickle of strength returned to me, so did my sanity, and I broke the embrace and stepped back. My hand swung automatically and struck him across the cheek. Annoyed, mostly at myself—although, he shared the blame, being so tempting and all when I was vulnerable—I hit him hard, and his face snapped to the side with the force of my blow. However, where another man would have taken offense at having a woman hit him, the vampire just laughed.

"Mysterious. Powerful. And playing hard to get. I must say you're intriguing me more and more."

It took a lot of willpower to resist the sexy drawl of his words. "Yeah, well, take your intrigue elsewhere. This woman is taken times two." And feeling kind of guilty that I'd enjoyed his embrace so much and, even worse, craved a continuation.

My declaration of my ménage situation caught him by surprise, and his eyebrows rose. Once again, though, instead of backing off, he grinned, showing his gleaming pair of fangs. "Well then, I look forward to becoming your third."

"A third? Oh, heck no. I've already got my hands," and pussy, "full as it is. So you can forget it."

"Forget a delicious enchantress?" He smiled. Oh, how he smiled and made my girly parts tingle. "Never. We will meet again. And you will crave my embrace."

Before I could say, when Hell freezes over—again—he swirled and a dark mist arose. When it cleared, the vampire, whose name I'd never gotten, had disappeared, leaving me with tingling lips, a wet pussy, and probably a flabbergasted look.

The pounding of feet had me whirling to face the new threat approaching, but to my relief and red-cheeked embarrassment, Auric was the one running toward me, a big blond panther at his side.

"Muriel!" he bellowed, his face creased in concern as he took in the prone bodies lying all about me.

He reached me, and I threw myself in the arms he opened wide. I buried myself in the protective comfort of his chest. Even kick-ass princesses liked to feel safe. Besides, I needed time to regain my equilibrium. Auric, however, didn't give me time to recover. I found myself being shaken.

"Of all the stupid things," he began ranting. "How many times do you have to be told not to go off on your own? How am I supposed to protect you if you take off on me? You could have been killed." While his voice and appearance sounded angry, I knew it hid fear, a fear that he would lose me. Guilt filled me. He was right. Once again, I'd gone with my first wild impulse instead of thinking and, even worse, trusting him.

However, feeling guilt and admitting to it were two different things. The words "I'm sorry" weren't something my dad had taught to me, and though I never wanted to hurt Auric because of my deep love for him, I also couldn't let him control all my actions. He pulled his macho act because he loved me. I did stupid shit because that was just who I was. Impulsive. Fearless. And not about to take his harangue quietly. "Don't you yell at me, mister."

"I will yell at you if I want to," he shouted. "What would possess you to take off like that?"

"Nothing possessed me." Unlike my poor neighbor's son who'd needed a priest to exorcise him. "I wanted some information so I came to find it."

"And this information couldn't wait for us to wake up properly and have breakfast?"

"Don't talk about food." My stomach roiled.

"But you love runny eggs and crispy bacon, or what about some nice hollandaise sauce dribbled over an English muffin."

I glared as my queasiness went to a new level. "You are a jerk."

"And you are a brat. I guess that makes us even." His expression softened. "Instead of fighting, tell me what happened."

"A couple of demons attacked me." Understatements were a specialty of mine.

"You killed all of them by yourself?" His note of incredulity miffed me a bit. He should have known by now how capable I was of taking care of myself.

"Do you see any demons standing? Are you saying I can't defend myself?" I went on the offensive—surely it wasn't lingering guilt making me snarky?

"Oh, come on, baby, I'm not a fucking idiot. You're unarmed and dressed in flip-flops. I doubt even superwoman could have taken on all these demons by herself and prevailed."

"I do have magic, remember?" I waggled my fingers.

"Your magic turns demons to dust. That's not what happened to this bunch." Auric swept a hand at the bodies David's cat was sniffing. He'd not said much in this fight, on account none of us understood meow and yowl, but I was good at understanding his purr when I scratched him behind the ears.

Lying at this point was probably useless. "Fine. I didn't kill these ones. But I did demolish the first bunch with my magic. Then, when the second group appeared, I thought I was toast until some vampire dude came to my aid and kicked the rest of their asses." And he'd kissed me, but I held that part back for the moment.

"A vampire came to your rescue? More like he was after your blood. Where is he? Did you kill him?

Did he touch you? Take your blood?" I shook my head wildly as Auric fired questions at me.

"He didn't bite me." I rolled my eyes as he made me tilt my chin to check my neck for marks.

His brow knitted. "Their kind doesn't act without reason. What did he want if he didn't take blood?"

He wanted to know what I was and then kissed me. However, that wasn't what I said aloud. "He didn't say. He just kicked some demon ass and then disappeared." Guilt squeezed me as I lied to my lover. But seriously, I was more afraid of telling him what had happened and seeing his disappointment in me. In retrospect, I realized the whole kiss thing was my fault. I should have fought my magical urge and never let the vampire near me.

"Let's go home." Auric tightened his arms around me. David, still in kitty form, and unable to change back unless he wanted to show off his naked parts, butted up against me.

Home? There he went trying to make me do things his way again. He really needed to read the memo I kept sending him that declared the world, and Hell, revolved around me and my wishes. I pushed away from Auric. "I am not going anywhere until I finish what I came to do."

I expected him to argue with me and order me back home like a bad little girl—who totally needed a spanking. Instead, he gave a curt nod. When I would have resumed walking toward the tower that was my destination, he swept me up, and I cuddled gratefully into his arms. My fallen angel knew how to treat a princess, and I knew how to reward him. I nibbled the underside of his jaw, but the teasing wasn't just for him. My magical battery was still pretty empty and needed some juice to fill it. Necking wasn't a seven-course sexual feast, but it fed me a little energy, which my magically dehydrated body absorbed.

As we neared our destination, I took in the details. The spooky-looking tower, tier upon tier of crumbling dark stone, was the home of Prune Face, my dad's most powerful mage who held the title Sorceress. The damned ones and demons also called her 'that soul-sucking bitch', but she'd earned my respect so I abstained from repeating it. On my last visit, I'd finally discovered her name, Nefertiti. It sounded familiar so I Googled it and found thousands of hits relating to an ancient Egyptian queen. Since time in Hell didn't necessary mean a person aged as they did on the mortal plane, I wasn't entirely surprised to discover a woman of her power was really freaking old. Yet even given her age, and even more ancient, cobwebbed pussy, the woman boasted of sexual escapades that would make even my succubus sister Bambi blush.

A part of me wondered if Nefertiti had always been a sexual deviant or if the magic that demanded feeding had turned her into one. I feared the answer. Would my nympho magic force me to bring more lovers into my circle and, even worse, tempt me into trying things better left in erotic books?

Would I be tempted to try new flavors? Say perhaps a dark, cold one? Even the insidious thought made me shiver, and poor Auric, he hugged me tighter, never knowing that it wasn't a chill that permeated my being, but desire. Desire for another, even as I already loved two.

Arriving at the cobbled walk to the tower, Auric let me down to stand on my own two feet. I regarded the square blocks set in a pattern and felt an urge to click my flip-flops and go home. Instead, I muttered, "Just follow the black brick road." Flanked by my men, the strong angel and the brave panther, we approached the sinister-looking abode.

It was times like these I really wished my life had a soundtrack. I mean, really, I could totally hear the ominous music as we climbed the stone steps, worn smooth from the passage of others before us. I could hear the hush in the chorus as I raised my fist to bang on the massive door banded in iron.

Knock. Knock. Knock.

I'd like to say it opened with a creak, the dark aperture beckoning with spooky ghostly fingers. Alas, my imagination was more vivid than reality. Without even a small squeak, the oversized door swung open, bright light spilled, beckoning warmly, and a butler, sporting curly blond hair—think Grecian hunk in a loin cloth—waved us in.

"Princess, you grace us with your delectable presence."

And he showed his appreciation of my delectable presence with a lift of his loincloth. Funny how much a fallen angel growling resembled a displeased panther.

Jealousy did my lovers good. A man, or in this case men, should never take their woman for granted. And, besides, the whole 'my woman' thing? Totally hot.

Being a smart girl, I kept my eyes on the butler's face instead of below his belt, more because I feared a jealous sorceress than anything else. "I'm here to see your mistress."

"But of course. My mistress has been expecting

you," the blond butler, with impressive abs, announced. He swept a hand, gesturing for us to enter the tower. We all stepped in. The door shut behind us, this time by a ghostly wind that did not impress me. My dad had pulled too many pranks on me growing up for me to be impressed. Some kids feared the monster under the bed. Mine had two.

As the butler turned to lead the way into the tower, Auric growled, as did David. The reason? The butler's pivot revealed that the loincloth, while covering the front, left the rear bare except for the thong disappearing between a pair of perfectly sculpted cheeks. Nice. Very nice.

"Think she'd give me a pair of those outfits to take home?" I teased.

"You will avert your eyes," Auric grumbled, his body stiff next to mine.

I couldn't help a moue of surprise. Auric actually forbidding me to look because of jealousy? Awesome. And strange. I mean, sure I expected some male posturing, that was natural, but to actually forbid me from even looking? So very, very strange. After all, here was a man who'd just about forced me to bring a second man into our relationship to give me the magic I needed. A man who got off on watching me suck and fuck David, and yet he didn't want me looking at another guy's ass? It just reinforced my initial impulse to hide the kiss with the vampire. *Jeez, if he's pissed 'cause I'm looking, he'd go ballistic if he found out about a lip lock. Hmmm, but I bet the after-fight sex would be fantastic.*

A furry body went slinking past us as David took point position behind the strutting buns of steel. I didn't hear a thing, but David must have done something—that or the butler had a fear of cats—because those already tight buttocks clenched up so tight I doubt we could have flossed them.

After what seemed like a maze of corridors and turns, stone passageways lit with smokeless torches and hung with tapestries depicting sex acts that involved way too many limbs, we arrived in what could only be classed as a harem.

As we walked into a cavernous chamber, which, compared to the rest of the place, appeared light and airy, I ogled in astonishment. I'll admit, in my bias, I'd expected to see lots of dark red velvet, a giant shag carpet, chains, and a monster-sized bed with an array of lubes alongside it.

Instead, there were high, arched windows letting in light, which had to be artificial given Hell's reddish glow. A huge fountain in the middle of the room bubbled; I especially liked its statue of a naked man peeing out of a massive marble cock. Divans, pillows, and chairs abounded, and while they varied in color, they all had one thing in common: comfort. Oh, and there was one other hugely noticeable aspect to the room—lots and lots of naked men.

Talk about eye-candy overload. I swear my tongue just about hung out of my mouth as I drooled at the vast array of naked flesh in every color imaginable and some that had to be artificial. I mean, seriously, there was a guy who was blue from head to toe, even his prick and balls.

A hand was clapped over my eyes, and I squealed. "Auric! What are you doing?"

"Protecting you from yourself," he announced in Neanderthal fashion.

Annoyed as I was at his jealous treatment, I'd admit I also found it hot. My fallen angel was usually the cool and collected one. To find him susceptible to such a human trait as jealousy simply endeared him to me even more.

"Auric, let her go." David's demand surprised me for two reasons. One, he never went against Auric's wishes that I knew of, and second, he must have shifted back, which meant he currently showed off his naked parts—parts I owned for my own personal visual enjoyment and use.

"You'd better be wearing some clothes," I sputtered as the heavy hand over my eyes lifted. I opened them to see David wearing a grin and nothing else. Not that he had anything to be ashamed of. His body, with its lean, rippled physique rivaled those in the room. However, I suddenly discovered that, while I didn't mind eyeballing Nefertiti's sex slaves, I wasn't so keen on returning the favor with my men.

I've never denied having a jealous nature. Hell, the last broad who'd tried to hit on Auric had worn a black eye for a week.

Ignoring their masculine chuckles, I strode over to a table set with delicacies and tore the tablecloth off it. Of course, I lacked the skill of an entertainer, and the dishes went crashing to the floor, not that I cared. I wrapped the length of fabric around David's hips while he regarded me with a smirk and crossed arms. I didn't like leaving his chest bare, but the only option would be to either use Auric's shirt, which would leave him half naked, or give him my shirt, which I doubted Auric would allow.

Mental note to self—*next time I come to Hell, I need to bring some spare clothes for situations like these.*

All the kerfuffle over clothing made me miss the arrival of our hostess.

"Lucifer's daughter, how kind of you to visit."

I whirled and then lost my tongue to shock. I'd recognized the voice as belonging to Prune Face, my father's mage, but the beautiful woman standing in front of me looked nothing like the crone I'd previously dealt with. Gone were the wrinkles and hunched form of the witch, replaced by a petite woman with long, glossy black hair, luminous tanned skin, and a nude figure that put all women to shame, and that made me wish for another tablecloth to cover her up with.

"What the fuck?" I finally managed to say. Eloquence, ever my enemy.

Nefertiti smiled, a slow, sensuous thing that made her large doe-like eyes glow. "When I work at the castle, I prefer my colleagues and assistants not be distracted, so I wear my true age. But at home, with my lovers, I prefer to revert back to my youth."

"It's a good look for you, really it is, but could you put some clothes on?"

Nefertiti laughed. "Considering whose daughter you are and the type of magic we share, you're awfully prudish."

"Not prudish, just murderously jealous."

"You would dare threaten me?" One perfect brow arched.

"It's not a threat but a promise."

For a moment, those eyes lost their alluring glow and promise. They narrowed. "You've got a lot of nerve coming into my home and giving orders."

"I've got tits of steel, too, and might I remind you I am a princess of Hell and you are a vassal of my father?"

"Is the little princess going to call her daddy?"

The mockery held just the right tone, and I couldn't help a grin, not a very nice one. "I don't need Daddy to fight my battles. And you would do well to remember that, one day, I will be the one running this joint."

"You forget your brother."

At that, we both laughed. I mean, really, Christopher didn't have the balls or inclination to truly embrace his role as the Antichrist and bringer of destruction. I, on the other hand, had just the right blend of bitch to get away with it. And Nefertiti knew it. "So, are you going to put some fucking clothes on, or are we going to tit wrestle to see who's the biggest bitch?"

"Your father raised you well. You'll do well in the battles to come." An enigmatic answer that wasn't as interesting as the fact that I'd won the battle of wills.

Good thing, too, given, in a fight, the sorceress

probably would have kicked my magically depleted ass.

Nefertiti snapped her fingers, and the half-naked dude who'd answered the door came running to drape a silken robe around her lush body, hiding her assets. As for my men, who'd stared at her instead of poking out their own eyes? I stomped on Auric's foot and kicked David in the shin. I'd punish them more later.

With her robe belted, Nefertiti turned and, with a wiggle that made me glower at my men in warning, led us to a table being hastily set by the fountain.

We sat down, and I opened my mouth to speak, but a sharp look from our hostess made me snap it shut.

"Not yet," she admonished. "Just because we are in Hell does not mean we shouldn't make a pretense of the niceties. Tea?"

Seriously?

Apparently seeing as how she poured some hot liquid into some fine china cups. The tannish beverage steamed, and I wrinkled my nose. "I don't suppose you have coffee? Maybe a latte?"

"You will drink the tea," said in a no-nonsense tone I chose not to object to. After all, I was here to ask for help, and given our somewhat rocky start, I might want to start acting a little nicer—while inwardly plotting evil because that was so much more fun.

Her butler offered us a platter of desserts, delectable, tiny cakes iced with finesse. No need to twist my arm where those were concerned. I took a pink one without hesitation. I had a sweet tooth, and biting into the creamy confection, I almost swooned.

"That is so good," I said with a taste-bud-felt moan.

"It should be. Frederick makes them from scratch. His secret is a fresh blend of *creams*."

The way she said cream made me choke, and I gulped down the hot tea laced with some kind of mint undertone.

Nefertiti laughed as I scowled at her through watering eyes.

"Ah, Muriel. You are so entertaining. The cream you fear would never be wasted on guests. That is a delicacy I reserve for myself."

I refused to feel sheepish, but I did allow relief to loosen the tension in my shoulders. "Can we cut out the bullshit? I didn't come here to see your naked boobs or to find out if you spit or swallow. I need some help."

"It's obvious you're here for help. Why else

would you visit unless you wanted to borrow my harem to increase your magic?"

Grrr.

"I see you are not the only one still plagued by foolish notions of jealousy. You and your men have much to learn."

"I know we do. That's why we're here."

"Have you finally decided to ask me for tips on creating even more potent magic? I can tell just by looking at you that you've yet to allow your men to truly fuck you. Why do you hesitate?"

I knew what she spoke of. A true sandwich, where one got my pussy and the other my ass. Call me old-fashioned, but in my book, asses were out holes, not in. "Our sex life is doing perfectly fine, thank you. I'm here about something else. My mother showed up, and she kind of dropped a bomb."

"Yes, I'd heard Mother Nature had returned," Nefertiti said with a nod. "Your father mentioned it when he called."

"Do you know my mother?" Blast my curiosity for wanting to know more.

"I recall her now that she's decided to reappear in your life." A moue of annoyance creased Nefertiti's face. "I am displeased to discover she had the power to hide away all memories of her."

"How is that possible?"

The sorceress shrugged. "There are many mysteries we have no answers to. Magic we cannot even imagine."

"That is really not reassuring."

"It wasn't meant to be. The truth is sometimes harsh."

"My dad hates the truth." With a passion actually.

"Yet, Lucifer knows without the truth there are no lies."

"Speaking of lies, Gaia told me something." Something I still didn't want to believe.

"She claims you are pregnant by both your lovers."

"That's impossible, right?" My anxiety sounded crystal clear, even to me.

"Nothing is impossible."

"Don't pull that bullshit with me. Making babies is biological. Sperm meets egg. That's the way it is. Not two tadpoles fertilize. Just one. Or, even better, how about none?" Because the whole idea of parenthood freaked me the fuck out.

Nefertiti held my gaze for a moment before

turning her head. "Auric and David, you will leave me alone with Muriel for a moment."

I expected Auric to tell her, in no certain terms, no fucking way, and he didn't disappoint. His arms crossed over his chest, and his face took on that stubborn expression I hated and adored.

"I'm not going anywhere."

"Such loyalty, and without the strength to back it," Nefertiti said with a cluck of her tongue. She snapped her fingers, and while I didn't hear her speak any magical words, the effect was obvious. Auric and David were picked up by an invisible hand and moved away.

A roar of rage left Auric, and he struggled against the invisible ties that bound him. David also squirmed, to no avail.

I glared at the sorceress. "Let them go. This instant."

"Stop whining like a child, Princess. Your lovers are not far and won't come to harm. Do you want answers?"

"Of course I do." But I didn't want to face those answers alone. I wanted Auric and David to hold my hand and reassure me that things would turn out all right. But that would be admitting I feared the truth.

I am not scared of anything. Anymore that was.

Now that the curse that had made me live in terror was gone, I'd promised myself to face life head-on, whether I liked it or not.

"If you want the truth, then you will have to do as I say."

Obeying wasn't a strong suit of mine. Annoyed, I drummed my fingers on the table. "Fine. You got them to leave, so now what?"

"First off, I need to examine you. Stand, please, and lift your shirt."

I arched a brow.

Nefertiti sighed and snapped her fingers. A curtain rose up around us, not a fabric one, more of a swirling mist, but it served as a privacy barrier. I stood and raised my shirt. The witch walked around me while I stared up at the ceiling, feeling like an idiot. I was also quite fascinated by the frescoes painted above me. Surely some of those naked pretzels were physically impossible?

I flinched when she placed her hands on my abdomen, not out of fear but because they were colder than freaking ice cubes.

"Holy fuck! Wear some gloves next time, would you?"

Nefertiti just clucked her tongue and continued to grope my tummy. Her hands slid up and cupped my boobs, and I couldn't help but blush, especially since my buds perked.

"Nice tits," she remarked with a tweak to my nipples.

"Hey!"

A smirk tilted her lips. "Prude." She stepped away from me and returned to her seat.

"Pervert," I muttered.

"Thank you."

And that was all she said. I waited for her to speak, but she just gave me an implacable stare.

Usually, I was good at this game, but today, impatience was my best friend. "So?"

"So what? You're pregnant. But I'm pretty sure you knew that before you came here."

Yeah, but now it was confirmed and scary. "And?"

"And what?"

I clenched my fists and reminded myself not to punch the woman who had answers. "Whose baby is it? Auric's or David's?"

The smile came slowly, and mirth danced in her eyes. "Both, of course, and growing much more rapidly than a human one would. Congrats, mommy."

My body suddenly heavy, I plopped onto the

chair and laid my head down on the table. I gripped the sides. I had to. It was that or swoon and fall off my chair. "Impossible. I mean, how the fuck can I be pregnant by two men? What are there like twins in there or something?"

"One child. A female."

A daughter? I didn't say anything for a moment as the knowledge sank in. "What's different about this baby other than the fact it's growing faster than normal?"

"Its power. I'd thought you were the most powerful child I'd ever met, but even though this fetus is the size of your thumb, the child you carry is already immensely powerful."

Well, that explained why my mother, the cow, wanted her. What I still didn't get was for what. "What should I do?" I mused the words aloud, not really expecting an answer, so when it came, it took me a minute to absorb it.

"Kill it. Kill it before it destroys us all," hissed Nefertiti.

I raised my head and gaped at her. "Abortion? Are you nuts? I mean I'm not like religious or anything, but still, you're talking about my baby here."

Sorrow darkened Nefertiti's eyes. "A child with

the potential to rend the world apart. Why do you think I sent the fathers away? Right now, you have the option to end this right now. I can remove the fetus from your womb and give you something to prevent any future accidents. This is too momentous to allow men and their pride to decide. The choice needs to be yours alone."

"You really think my having a baby would be that bad?"

"My power doesn't lie in foretelling the future, but even I can sense the danger. This child could destroy us. Destroy you."

"Could? You keep saying could, so this isn't a concrete thing. There's a possibility you're wrong."

Nefertiti grudgingly nodded.

"So I raise her to be a good girl who learns that destroying the world is bad. In other words, teach her the difference between right and wrong." The irony of my words didn't escape either of us, and I blamed stress for my hysterical laughter.

"You've asked my opinion. What you do now is up to you, but keep in mind, once this child is born, there will be no turning back. Are you prepared to fight to keep her safe? And, if she treads down a path of darkness, to see her destroy everything you love?"

A truly maternal mother would have instantly

said yes, but foreboding, dark and cold, settled on me, and I knew to speak those words would somehow affect the course of the future. A future I didn't yet understand or foresee.

I avoided answering. For now I'd stick my head in the sand like an ostrich and face this dilemma once I'd had time to mull it over.

Nefertiti sighed. "Fool. If you change your mind, come see me but don't wait too long. At the rate this child is growing, you may not have as much time as you think."

Great, I had a ticking time bomb in my stomach, and I wondered if that meant I'd start craving really weird pregnant shit like pickles and ice cream, plutonium and gunpowder. My imagination ran wild in an attempt to make me smile, but nothing about this situation was amusing.

Nefertiti dropped the privacy curtain, and instead of finding my men close by, anxiously waiting for the verdict, I saw them off in a huddle with several of Nefertiti's lovers.

"Do you seriously bang all these guys?" I asked in curiosity. I mean we were talking about a lot of men here.

"Well, I can take three at a time, and sometimes,

if I'm feeling particularly drained, I'll have those taking me being fucked themselves."

The mental image was disturbing. I liked my two men, but somehow I didn't think I'd ever be comfortable with them touching each other. In my world, it was all about me and my pleasure. "I think I'll stick to my vanilla fun."

"Party pooper. You haven't had a true threesome until you've been sandwiched. You really should try it sometime."

Yeah, when hell freezes over. Oops. That had already happened. I really needed to come up with a new expression.

My men, seeing me tapping my foot impatiently, finally broke from their confab with the naked men and strode over to me. I wanted to go home, like right this instant, but lacked the magical oomph at the moment to call a portal. Not that I could have in Nefertiti's tower. She had some kick-ass shields in place, almost as good as my dad's.

I linked my arms into those of both my men, and with me between them, we left. I could feel their curiosity, their burning need to ask what had happened. But I couldn't tell them. Not yet.

The revelations spinning in my head were hard

to absorb. I was glad they didn't ask me anything. I needed to figure out how much to tell them.

Planning to lie? Maybe. I knew Auric would expect me to be one hundred percent honest. The problem was I didn't know what he'd think of Nefertiti's advice to abort. Since he was still in many ways an angel, my first thought was he'd say no way. Some habits died hard, and even though I didn't go to church or read the Bible, and while I'd never actually met him, I knew Uncle God didn't approve of abortion at all. But given the troubles my dad had with God's religious zealots when that human woman had conceived my brother, the Antichrist, I also realized apparently, in certain situations, the rules could sometimes be bent.

On the flip side, given Auric's propensity to want to save the world, I couldn't actually be sure he wouldn't agree with Nefertiti that the babe needed to go. He was the type to sacrifice one person for the greater good of humanity. Could I ever forgive him if he made that choice for me?

And then there was David. Once upon a time, he'd been such a docile kitty, but now that he'd taken up permanent residence in my life and heart, the jerk had grown a backbone. Who knew what he'd want? I just hoped the half-kitty baby in my tummy didn't grow claws and tear its way out. Curse you, *Alien*! Some things could never be forgotten.

Just like I couldn't forget Nefertiti's claim. Would my child destroy the world? Could I let her? Who got to make that choice?

Selfish or not, I didn't know if I wanted my lovers making the decision for me. This was, after all, my body, my baby, and, in my view, my choice. The real question was, would I let them argue their case before I decided?

We made it back home, and I still hadn't come any closer to an answer. I could smell an interrogation coming just by looking into Auric's eyes, but I didn't want to speak yet, not with words anyway. I threw myself into his arms and raised my lips for a kiss. I wanted, make that needed, skin-to-skin contact, needed one last time of mindless pleasure before I dealt with reality.

I loved the way they both read my mood, or smelled my desire, for only moments later we toppled into our really large bed, naked. David pressed in from the back, his mouth latching onto my neck and sucking while his cock pulsed against my backside. Auric claimed my front, his lips melded to mine while his cock pressed between us, hard and hot against my lower belly.

David raised my hips and lowered me onto Auric's cock. I threw my head back, enjoying the feel of him inside me. I rocked on him while David nibbled on my neck from behind, his large hands cupping my breasts and tweaking my nipples. David pushed me down, and Auric's lips caught mine in a sweet kiss that made me forget everything but the pleasure invading my body. David kissed his way down my back to my buttocks. His hands spread my cheeks, and he continued to lick his way down the crevice of my ass until he reached my rosette. I tore my mouth from Auric's and tried to turn to see David so I could ask him what the fuck he thought he was doing, but Auric grabbed my face and forced me back.

David licked my out hole, a strange sensation for sure that made me squirm, which in turn drove Auric's cock deeper into me. Auric kept trying to distract me with his tongue, but it wasn't until David's odd licking stopped that I relaxed, only to tense up a moment later when a finger probed at my anus. Auric kept my face locked to his mouth so I couldn't mouth my protest. David pushed at my tight ring with his finger but made little headway. So the jerk changed tactics. He brought his other hand around to my front and pinched my clit.

I bucked, and he used that moment to penetrate my back hole with his digit. The strange sensation mixed with his pinching and rubbing of my clit sent me into a roaring climax that had all my vaginal muscles squeezing deliciously, forcing Auric to jet his cream into me with a grunt.

My orgasmic waves hadn't stopped when I found myself flipped onto my back, my legs spread wide so David could take his turn plowing me. The renewed fucking stimulated my still quivering channel and thrust me into a second orgasm that milked David dry.

Magic replenished, I lay there for a moment recuperating, my body smooshed on either side by my lovers.

Then I let them have it. I jumped up from between them and stood over them like some glorious fifty-foot-tall naked woman "What the hell do you think you were doing?" I asked with a glare.

David shrugged. "We were talking to Nefertiti's lovers about some new stuff to try in the bedroom."

I admit that admission stole my tongue for a moment. "You what?" I sputtered. Oh fuck, what kind of perverted shit had they convinced my boys to do?

Auric tucked his hands behind his head and

grinned at me unabashedly. "You can stop acting all indignant. I know you liked it. The proof is drying on my cock." He kicked my legs out from under me and ensured I landed on his body.

With his arms wrapped around me, I found it hard to hold on to my anger. "A little bit of warning next time," I grumbled good-naturedly. Staying pissed seemed counterproductive, given their goal to pleasure me in new and wonderful ways.

"Warning is for pussies."

I couldn't help a groan. "Did you really just quote my dad?"

The chest under my cheek rumbled as he laughed. "I have to admit he's got some pretty colorful expressions."

"He's corrupting you."

"And is that such a bad thing?" Auric's big hand cupped my bare ass cheek.

David groped the other. "If this is what corruption is like, then I'm ready for more."

"What am I going to do with you?"

I joined them in laughing when they both said, "Do us."

When the mirth died down, I could almost feel the shift in the mood from light to somber. Here it came, the moment I dreaded.

"When are you going to tell us what the sorceress said?" Auric asked.

Stall. Pull a fire alarm. Do anything but tell them. I needed an excuse and found it easily when I caught a whiff of brimstone, sweat, and utter ick. "I'll tell you, but I need a shower first."

An obvious delaying tactic, yet a needed one. I wanted more time to think over what I'd learned. However, time didn't clarify the situation. A stupidly long hot shower didn't either. The minutes I spent brushing my teeth and then flossing them didn't provide a handy escape or a feasible reply to their query.

I didn't know what to tell them.

When I ran out of things to do, I faked fatigue, not entirely untrue, given I'd sneaked out of bed early. To my relief, they let me crawl under the covers, and even tucked me in, but I knew I couldn't avoid the questions forever, even if I was prepared to run from the answers.

CHAPTER THREE

*H*ours later, I woke to find the late afternoon sun bathing the loft. I played possum in bed, listening to the sounds of my guys cooking some grub—lucky me—and listening to the sports channel.

Although the smoky scent of bacon crisping tempted me, I stayed hidden under the covers, not ready to deal with them and their inevitable curiosity. I expected, make that knew, Auric would press me for details. I just didn't know how much to tell him. I needed to plan my next move and decide how I felt about everything that had occurred in the last twenty-four hours. My emotions were riding the roller coaster of life, and the dips and rushing speed were starting to make me nauseous. I wondered if I could avoid reality altogether until it was time to go to work.

Plotting dishonesty. I was truly turning into my father's daughter, and the thought didn't please me at all. Auric and David deserved better from me.

The quiet hum of the television abruptly ended. I heard the door to the apartment open and shut. Silence reigned for several minutes, and I blew out a noisy breath.

"Faker."

"Eep!" Startled, I had a totally girly moment and screamed. I peeked out from under the covers and saw Auric standing beside the bed with his arms crossed. Bloody man moved as quietly as my damned cat.

"Now that you're done pretending to sleep, going to tell me what's going on?"

"I don't suppose we could have sex instead?" My hopeful question lightened his expression a touch.

"Time to stop hiding, baby."

"Ugh. Don't use that word." What was once a term of endearment now served only to remind me of my predicament.

"You need to talk to me, Muriel." He sat on the edge of the bed, his green eyes soft as spring grass.

"What did Nefertiti tell you? And why does it have you so freaked out?"

Sitting up in bed, I intentionally let the sheet fall, but even the display of my fabulous bosom didn't veer his intent stare away. I pouted and knew I could hide my secret no longer. "I'm pregnant."

I waited for the shock, disbelief. Instead, I got an arched brow. "And? I think we already came to that conclusion. Now tell me the part I don't know."

"It's a g-g-girl." Tears pricked my eyes, and seconds later, I sobbed noisily against his chest while his arms held me in a hug tight enough to crush a mortal's ribs.

It was mortifying. Humiliating. Princesses of Hell didn't cry, they made other people cry, and yet, there I was sobbing like a weak ninny. The shame of it couldn't stem the tears though. And Auric's gentle rubbing of my back and soothing tone didn't help.

"Don't cry, Muri. You're pregnant, not dying. I know it's sooner than expected, but we'll work something out. David and I aren't going anywhere, although we'll probably have to move. What do you think of selling the loft and buying a house? Hell, if we get a big enough place with a gated property, you can even get one of those damned hellhounds for the baby if you want. Just please don't cry."

His acceptance of my pregnancy just made it worse. I wailed louder. "You...you don't understand," I said, hiccupping through my tears. "The baby is growing like superfast, and...and it's already like majorly powerful."

"So she's special, just like her mother," he placated, stroking my hair.

His understanding made something snap in me, and I tried to push away, only he wouldn't let me. So I used words as my weapon. "Stop being so fucking nice about this. You have no idea what you're saying."

"So tell me. Tell me why you've been acting so strange since your talk with Nefertiti."

"You don't want to know the truth."

"And yet, you're going to tell anyway," was his firm rejoinder.

He wanted the truth? I'd give him the ugly, unvarnished truth. "The baby inside me is not human. Nor demon. Nor anything this world has ever seen. She's powerful, so very powerful, enough that she has the potential to destroy the world and everyone in it." I spat the words out in a rush, and Auric's body went still.

"Um, what did you just say?"

"The baby inside me isn't human."

"I meant the part after that, Muri."

I sighed, and my shoulders sagged in defeat. I gave him the unvarnished truth. I loved Auric. How could I do any less? "Nefertiti thinks I should abort because the baby might cause Armageddon all on her own."

"Holy shit, Muriel. Why the fuck didn't you tell me this yesterday?" He pulled away from me and stood. However, news of this kind required action, and he paced in front of the bed, his face and body taut. "This is bloody serious, Muri. I can't believe you didn't tell me sooner. I thought it was too early in your pregnancy for the crone to tell you anything and that's why you kept quiet. Shit." He scrubbed a hand through his hair. "Now that I know, we need to make plans."

"I know," I sniffled. "And I wanted to tell you, but see, I know you're like the world's champion, and I already know what you're going to say. The fate of one isn't worth the lives of many, but...but I think I want this baby, Auric." It wasn't until I said it aloud that I truly realized it.

Yes, I wanted this baby, this child created of love, a part of me and Auric and David. I just didn't know if I had the strength to fight my lovers and everyone else who it seemed would want to kill her.

Auric spun on his heel and regarded me with green eyes that blazed in fury. "Back up a second. I don't believe you. Did you really think I'd ask you to kill our child? Are your pregnancy hormones driving you out of your fucking mind, woman? I would never, ever, do that to you. To our daughter."

My heart stopped. Had I heard him right? Had he understood what this child might be capable of? "You mean you don't want me to get rid of the baby?"

"No!" He bellowed the word.

I had to ask, though, to ensure there was no misunderstanding. "Are you sure? What if she ends up being some crawling nuclear weapon in a pink bow?"

Auric's smile was filled with such tenderness and love I think I would have faced the Legion of Hell single-handed to prove I was worthy of it. "When I said we needed to make plans, I meant to protect you and our unborn child. I care about the fate of the world, but I love you more. This child, even if shared with David, is ours. If she has powers, then we will teach her to use them with compassion. A child is the product of her parents. And really, could she have a more wonderful mother?"

My eyes brimmed, even as my lips curled into a

smile so wide my face almost split. "You are the most awesomest man ever, and I am the luckiest woman alive."

This time when we hugged it was for more than comfort. I tore at his annoying clothes, ripping them from him in my haste. He danced out of my reach, though, and wagged a finger at me. "Much as I'd enjoy that, we're not done talking. We still haven't addressed the whole mommy issue."

"I thought you said I'd be a great mom?" I replied, my sulky tone going well with my jutting lower lip.

"You will be. I wasn't talking about you though. I meant your mother, Gaia."

I pouted for real at her name. "Do we have to talk about her?" Talk about a downer.

Auric shook his head. "You can't keep avoiding her existence, Muri. I don't expect you to have a warm, fuzzy relationship with her or invite her to Thanksgiving dinner, given what she's done. But we need to discuss her because I'm sure you haven't forgotten what she said. While Nefertiti thinks you should abort, Gaia, on the other hand, wants us to hand the baby over."

"Like fuck," I spat.

"Exactly." He nodded. "But her request means

she's tipped her hand, and I, for one, would like to know more about why she wants our child. I also want to discover if we need to worry about her trying to kidnap the child once it's born."

"Just kill her now and get it over with." In my life, decisions were simple.

Auric blew out a breath. "I know you're upset with her for abandoning you, so am I actually, but we can't just kill her. There could be severe repercussions for destroying Mother Earth after all."

"Great. Take her side," I grumbled as I crossed my arms.

"I am not taking her side. She touches one hair on your head or our child's and I'll kill her without a second thought. And, you seem to have forgotten, in our battle with Gabriel, the other power pulling the strings of his minion puppets knew who your mother was. Don't you think we should, at the least, question your mother about whom this being is? Find out all the facts before we make a decision and act?"

I rolled my eyes. "You and your facts. Fine. She lives for now. But here's one fact you haven't clued in on. I'm horny and have less than an hour before I need to get to work. So do you mind cutting the talk and getting busy over here?"

Some might say laughter was the best remedy. I

begged to differ. Sex—the sweaty, emotionally charged kind—was much, much better.

Looking into Auric's eyes as he made love to me made me realize that, no matter what the future held, I wouldn't face it alone. And when my orgasm crashed over me in a sensual wave that made me writhe, I clutched him to me tightly in an attempt to fight the darkness I sensed hovering on the horizon. A foreboding that seemed to mock my brave attempt to fool myself.

We were basking in the afterglow when I remembered something I'd forgotten from the previous day's attack. A tidbit of knowledge that Auric needed to know.

"Azazel is up to his tricks again."

"What?" Auric rolled himself on top of me and peered down with concern. "Explain."

"The demons who attacked me yesterday did so on his orders. Somehow, even though he's supposed to be under guard and tortured daily, he's found a way to give his lackeys orders." And that meant whoever controlled Azazel, that mysterious power who'd fucked with my life a lot recently, had access to him, too. I wondered if my dad suspected, but I wondered even more just who in blazes this superpower was. I wasn't naive enough to think my dad,

Uncle God, and my mother were the only powerful entities around. There were many planes of existence. Heaven, Hell, and Earth were just the ones I was most familiar with. Who knew what existed out there in Limbo, space, and elsewhere? It could have been the one-eyed, four-armed, soaring, pink people eaters pulling the strings and entertaining themselves at our expense. However, while the identity of Azazel's true master interested me, I didn't allow it to sway my opinion about Azazel. The demon needed to die.

"He won't be giving fucking orders for much longer," Auric growled, reading my mind. He slipped out of bed to pull on some clothes.

I loved it when he got all protective. I rolled on my stomach and watched him hide his yummy flesh with clothing—wrapping paper, as I called it—that always seemed to beg to be torn off. "What are you going to do?"

"Tear his limbs from him one at a time and then finish him off permanently."

Say what you would, when my consort went all tough-ass alpha, it was freaking hot. "Mmm, say that again," I purred.

Auric gazed back at me, and I stretched with a lazy smile that said, without words, I was his for the taking. He chuckled and shook his head. "Woman, you are some kind of sexy."

He leaned over and kissed me, his hard lips claiming mine in a possessive embrace that made me think we'd embark on round two. However, Auric was ever the responsible one. He pulled back and ran a finger down my bare torso. "Keep that thought for later, after I come back from ripping that fucking demon a new one."

"I'll keep you to that promise. Now, as to killing the bastard, you'd better speak to my dad first and make sure he takes off his punishment spell or he'll just come back to life."

While the damned could suffer eternal torture and never die, only the abyss could end them permanently. Demons, on the other hand, were mortal. In order to punish them and not have them die before my dad was satisfied, he placed a spell on them that essentially rendered them immortal. I wasn't sure how it all worked, but I knew Auric would need to have it removed to take care of Azazel once and for all. I just wished I didn't have to go to work. I would have enjoyed watching Auric go medieval on his demonic ass.

"So does this mean I'm going to work by myself?" I asked, even as I knew the answer.

"You wish," he scoffed. "We both know the streets are safer if one of us is with you."

I blew him a raspberry then squealed as he dove on me and gave me one right back against my tummy.

I screamed and giggled at the loud, wet noise, only to feel my mirth die when he laid his cheek against the soft skin of my stomach. I stroked his lustrous, dark hair.

"I'll protect you both," he whispered. "My two precious girls."

Damned dust in my eyes made them water, had to be because I sure as hell wasn't crying again.

CHAPTER FOUR

I showered, unfortunately alone. Upon emerging from the steamy bathroom, I found Auric gone and David lounging on the couch. He waved a brown paper bag at me with a familiar coffee shop logo. "Hey, prego, want a donut?"

I thought about taking offense at his new nickname for me, but I found myself salivating when he pulled out a chocolate-covered Boston crème. He waved it in front of me with a teasing smile. I dove and grabbed at the treat. He used that as his opportunity to snag me and snuggle me onto his lap. I munched happily as he nuzzled my neck.

"Auric told me everything."

I stiffened, but didn't reply. I'd planned to have a talk with him as well, seeing how the whole baby scenario concerned him, too. My discomfort stemmed more from the two-daddy concept, which still kind of wigged me out. I mean, would our child come out with one green eye and one blue like the daddies? I wanted a daughter, not a husky.

He hugged me tightly. "I just wanted you to hear it from me that, no matter what, I'm with you. Even when you get as fat and round as a giant pumpkin, I'll still love you." That earned him a jab in the ribs, which made him chuckle. "And when it comes to our little girl, I'll lay down my life before I'll let anyone touch her."

"Even if she wants to rule the world?"

He shrugged. "If my baby girl wants it, then my baby girl will have it."

The damned dust returned. My eyes teared up, and I threw my arms around David's neck as I sobbed. "I love you, too, you giant furball."

These damned hormones were turning me into a wailing damsel, but at least my men didn't seem bothered. If this kept up though, I'd have to invest in a case of waterproof mascara. Raccoon face was not an attractive look for anyone.

"Enough blubbering, my lazy-ass princess. We need to get to work."

I glared at David as he dumped me off his lap

and then slapped my buttocks to get me moving. "Whatever happened to the nice, shy guy I met?"

"He fell in love with a smart-mouthed hottie whose daddy makes Charles Manson look like a cuddly bunny rabbit. Besides, I was always like this. You just never noticed because I was always tongue-tied and in awe of your formidable assets when around you." He mimed a pair of huge jugs, and I almost bit my tongue in shock.

"Shy, my ass," I muttered as I grabbed my purse.

"What's that? Did you say we could finally take you up the ass? Woo! Wait until I tell Auric."

I growled even as I giggled. "Pig! My ass is off-limits. Don't make me ground you from my pussy, too."

David snagged me in his implacable grip and grinned down at me. "You are so cute when you're annoyed." David kissed me and kissed me again.

In the end we were late getting to work as he showed me with his tongue, and then with his cock, just how cute I was. I already knew, but saw no harm in letting him prove it to me in such a pleasurable fashion.

Upon entering my bar, I noted Charon sat at his usual spot. I arched a brow at him. "Gee, make your-self at home why don't you?" My dad's oldest friend

—and I meant old—lifted his cowled head and peered at me. Or so I assumed. No one ever saw Charon's face. He had held the position of ferryman of souls on the River Styx for as long as anyone could remember. While he scared the crap out of most people, I adored him and considered him an honorary uncle. But loving him didn't mean I'd ever seen exactly what he hid under his head-to-toe robe. I'd often wondered if he took the robe off to make love to his wife or if he just lifted it up to plow her. Welcome to my mind, a sick yet interesting place that never gave me a dull moment.

Charon growled. "Don't start with me, Muriel. It was a tough day on the Styx."

"Uh-oh. What did your boy do now?" Charon's son, while attempting to follow in his father's footsteps—if he had feet—wasn't quite succeeding. Between losing the oars and putting a hole in the boat on previous occasions, I wondered what was left for him to sabotage.

"Adexios tipped the boat. Tipped it!" Charon almost roared. "It's bloody flat-bottomed. Hell, even the Styx monsters haven't managed to dump it, and my boy somehow manages to do it all on his own."

"Well, I hope the passengers were wearing life

jackets," I said brightly. I tried not to snicker, really I did, but I failed and laughed so hard I snorted.

"I'm glad you think that's so funny, considering one of the dunkees wasn't recovered."

I shrugged as I wiped down the bar. "My dad will find the lost soul eventually. It's not like they can drown."

"It wasn't a soul, but your friend, Azazel."

I froze and leaned my hands on the bar as I faced Charon. "Oh, you've got to be fucking kidding me. What the fuck was Azazel doing on the boat?"

"Your father was having him moved closer to the castle in preparation for a formal execution."

"Why didn't I know about it?" Dad should have known by now I didn't like secrets.

"It was supposed to be the crowning surprise at your birthday celebration."

The news of my upcoming party should have sent me into a tizzy. Instead, more serious thoughts took precedence. "Why the fuck was your idiot son in charge of the boat? Shouldn't that have been your job?" I yelled and felt bad when Charon actually flinched from me. A first...look at me starting to get a reputation for being badass. My dad would totally blow a gasket in jealousy.

"We're still trying to figure out how that

happened. My son doesn't remember a damned thing about the whole incident and neither do any of the other passengers."

I slapped my forehead. "Ah, fuck. Auric's on his way to Dad's to get the spell taken off Azazel so he can kill him. He's not going to be happy when he finds out Azazel is on the loose." I dove on my phone and dialed my special number to Hades. 666-666-666-666... My dad's humor knew no bounds.

The phone rang and rang and rang some more before getting picked up.

"Hell's palace, how may we damn you?" Pokie, my dad's steward, answered, sounding flustered. Judging by the yelling and cursing in the background, recognizable as my dad and my consort, I could see why he might find himself a little frazzled.

"I take it they heard about Azazel escaping?"

"You think?" Pokie sighed. "Sorry for sounding snarky. They've been at this for a while now and I've run out of weed to smoke, and ear plugs."

"Put me on speakerphone." I drummed my fingers on the bar as I waited for Pokie to turn on the intercom. As soon as it clicked, I did my thing. "Hey, dumbasses. Stop fucking yelling at each other like bloody idiots and figure out where Azazel's evil ass is. I'm pregnant, remember, and not in the mood for this shit. Oh, and Auric, when you pop your ass back to this bar to protect me, you'd better bring some of Cook's famous jalapeño pie. Baby's hungry."

I didn't wait for a response. I hung up. The princess had spoken.

My glare stifled the laughter in the bar. I'd recently given up trying to keep my parentage a secret. Not that it accorded me more respect from regulars, but at least, now, the damned assassins knew where to come looking. Kicking their asses helped keep me in shape and kept my boys on their toes.

I threw myself into my work, trying not to let thoughts of Azazel on the loose bother me. Him I could handle with one hand tied behind my back. My growling stomach, on the other hand, was driving me insane.

Auric showed up about an hour later, the picture of calm. He handed me a heavy basket filled to the brim with goodies. As I munched with great appetite, he related to David and me things we already knew, like Azazel's escape, and things we didn't, like the major demon hunt going on for his capture.

"Your dad's also sending us one of his hunters, just back from the wild, for added protection."

"More bodyguards?" I restrained a sigh. I didn't

have just myself to think of anymore. Look at me thinking of the baby first. *Hey, maybe this mommy thing won't be so bad after all.* As I peered into the empty basket though, I did find myself worrying about my waistline. *At the rate I'm eating, I'll need my own zip code soon.*

Business in my bar, Nexus, resumed, albeit more quietly now with Auric present. Most nights he just popped in and out as he went about his mysterious errands. I joked he was on a quest to save the world, but in truth, I never quite knew what he was up to. I trusted him, which, given the deceit in my life, was practically a miracle. But with Auric, I knew I didn't need to put spyware on his phone or have him followed. He loved me, and that was all I needed to know.

The evening passed in familiar comfort with patrons coming and going. They drank and filled my pockets with their ill-earned money, the best kind.

About an hour before closing, the main door opened, and a cool breeze wafted over me, waking my magic's hunger.

Something yummy this way comes. My body practically hummed with excitement. What the fuck? I turned to see what made my magical leech stretch and saw a familiar handsome dude.

Fang Boy had found me, and elation battled with panic. If I'd been behind the bar, I would have simply slipped into the back and avoided him. But out in the open, setting up the karaoke machine for the next night, I was stuck. A hide and seek player without a spot to hide. In other words, a loser about to get caught. Karma was such a bitch, aunt or not.

With a smile that made my tummy tingle in ways that made me feel guilty, the vamp headed toward me, a dark presence that caught the attention of all the women in the bar and the male demon dressed as one—I tended to attract a wide gamut of patrons. But that was not the only attention he drew. Before I knew it, my men flanked me, my fallen angel on one side and my bristling kitty on the other. It would have been hot if not for the upcoming and totally predictable testosterone match.

Personally, I cringed, but my libido screamed, "Take off your clothes, boys, before you start fighting!" What could I say? Even in the midst of a crisis, my slutty side thought ahead.

Fangalicious smiled at me, and I really wished for a hole to open up beneath me and swallow me whole before my dirty, and yet titillating secret, came out. I squirmed as my cheeks blushed in guilt. Silly me, I should have probably admitted the accidental kiss to my boys, but then I would have to admit I enjoyed it—a lot. And that would have opened a ginormous can of worms.

Or so I thought. I mean I was happy with my boys. The sex was freaking amazing, and since my talk with Nefertiti, and David's poke play with my behind, I was even contemplating letting them visit my forbidden cave. Don't laugh. That was a big thing for me, given the persisting feelings I had about inserting objects into exit holes.

The babble in my mind provided a great distraction, but it didn't stop the inevitable.

"We meet again, oh mysterious one," the vampire said with a low bow while his eyes raked me from head to toe. Did I mention it felt like he stripped me of clothes and caressed me while he did it?

"What are you doing here?" I asked.

"Looking for you."

Heart-stopping words. Also words that could get a vamp killed.

"Who the fuck are you?" Auric growled. Strong words from my consort, who was usually the diplomatic one. For a man who shared me with his best friend, he was showing a lot of uncharacteristic jealousy lately.

"Ah, you must be the two men she spoke of after

telling me I couldn't kiss her again." The dude obviously had a death wish, although my libido screamed, *oh yeah, baby and that was one helluva kiss.*

It was too much to hope that Auric hadn't caught what Fangalicious said.

"Did the vampire kiss you?" Auric asked through gritted teeth.

"Um, kind of," I admitted in a tiny voice.

Apparently, Auric just wanted confirmation before acting. I slapped my hand to my forehead as Auric dove onto the vamp and David burst out of his clothes, letting his panther take over. The three male bodies crashed together in a violent huddle that really would have provided more visual fun had they worn fewer clothes.

Perfume preceded Bambi's arrival at my side. "Goodness. You really are racing to catch up to me, aren't you? Am I going to have to fight to keep my title of Greatest Slut Ever?"

I thought of her many trophies consisting of numerous naked bodies contorted in positions that all had one thing in common—cocks in holes. "No, thanks. It would seem my men have reverted back to cavemen and think they need to thump their chests and beat others to prove themselves top alpha."

"Aren't you going to stop them?"

I glared at the tussling boys. "Why? Maybe if they smack each other enough they'll knock some sense into each other." Annoyed, and still feeling guilty—a feeling I was unused to, given I was usually rewarded for sin—I walked away from the problem, dragging my sister after me.

I slammed the door to my private office and flopped onto my couch.

"Spill it, lamb," Bambi demanded as she sat on the desk.

I made to avert my eyes because usually Bambi sitting at eye level was uncomfortable due to her lack of undergarments. But I did a double take as I took in what she wore.

"Pants? Are you actually wearing pants, and not just any pants, but slacks?" My jaw dropped, and I felt a sudden urge to call Hell and see if it had frozen over again. The only pants I'd ever seen my sister wear were the indecent kind. These loose slacks with the plain blue blouse and low-heeled shoes were wrong somehow. "What the fuck is up with the June Cleaver wardrobe?"

My sister, succubus and award-winning slut, blushed. "I met someone. Someone special."

"That's awesome," I congratulated her, jumping

up to hug her. "But what's that got to do with the clothes?"

"It throws him completely off balance to see me dressed demurely." Bambi grinned with a familiar salacious twinkle, and I laughed.

"Oh, that is so evil. I love it. So when do I get to meet the stud who makes you wear panties?" It warmed my heart to know my sister had found herself a man who made her happy.

"You already know him, but I don't want to say who yet. I'm not ready."

"Does he know what you are?"

Bambi nodded. "Yeah, he knows I'm a succubus, and that's kind of a problem. He's kind of human. Not one hundred percent, but enough I've got to be careful."

More than careful. Bambi needed soul essence, and while she could sip from humans, she couldn't take too often lest she accidentally kill or render that person soulless. Ghouls were such a pain to hunt and destroy.

"Are you doing to introduce him to Dad?"

A grimace creased her perfect features. "Ugh. No. Not yet. I'd say never, but we all know what happens when you keep a secret from him."

Yeah, he'd taken out a billboard and let all of

Hell know Muriel was crushing on that hot dude in grade twelve. It took her breaking his nose for the snickers to stop.

"Good luck if you guys manage to make it to the next level." When your father was The Devil, introducing boyfriends could end up interesting if they survived the experience.

"Enough about me. Care to explain what's up with the boys out front?"

"Gee, and here I thought you'd be more interested in the fact you're about to become an aunt."

Bambi squealed and almost took us both to the floor when she threw herself on me for an enthusiastic hug. "My little lamb is going to be a mommy." She sniffed back tears.

"Yeah, well, first I've got to survive the pregnancy."

Concern dried her eyes. "Are you okay? Is there any reason to worry?"

I told her about my mother's visit and my talk with Nefertiti, and I even admitted to the kiss I'd shared with Fang Boy. Bambi's eyes grew wider and wider.

"Damn, lamb. You just never do things by halves, do you?"

I smiled and shrugged. "Welcome to my fucked-up life."

"Well, I think you made the right decision to keep the babe. It's what happened when your mother got pregnant with you, after all."

"What!"

Bambi slapped a hand over her mouth. "You didn't hear me say that."

"Did too. Spill it."

"Well, see, it's the oddest thing. I hadn't even remembered you had a mother until you, like, talked about her. Now, though, it's as if I have all these memories, not many mind you, but the one that sticks out is one from when I was a child. I was playing in the lab, hiding from the other girls who didn't play nice with me 'cause I was prettier. Your mother came in, already talking with Nefertiti. I didn't get the whole conversation, but I do recall Nef telling your mom the baby she carried was dangerous. And your mother just shrugged and said, 'So what? She's mine, and I'm keeping her'."

It annoyed me that this knowledge made my plan to kill my mother shift. So, she'd cared about me at one point. It still didn't excuse her behavior. Curiosity made me wonder if perhaps I should find out more about what had happened so many years ago. If I didn't like the answer, I could still kill the bitch.

"Well, she didn't keep that promise, did she?" I replied bitterly. "In the end she might not have killed me, but she did dump me like unwanted garbage." Damned hormones. My eyes glistened, and I dug my nails into my hands, using the pain to veer my thoughts.

"Oh, little lamb. If she hadn't, I would have never known you and loved you."

I smiled tremulously at my sister. People could say what they wanted about her, but slut or not, she had a heart of gold, and I loved her dearly. "And sappy shit like that is why this baby's middle name is going to be Bambi."

We hugged tightly, both crying like the biggest saps. Then we had a makeup repair session. Coon eyes aren't sexy unless you're into the Goth look. Seeing as how I wore pink, a cleaning and reapplication was in order.

Face back on straight, I had one more question before we went back to face the bruises and black eyes I was sure my men sported. "Bambi, does having, um, sex, you know in the, um—" I couldn't say it, so I mimed it, my hand pointing to my butt.

"Anal sex feels great if done right," she said,

rolling her eyes. "Jeez, lamb, you can be such a prude sometimes. Don't tell me you've never done it? You have two lovers. You mean to tell me you've denied yourself and them that pleasure?"

My blush said it all.

"What are you waiting for? Let the poor boys have some fun. Keep in mind I'm not saying just let them drive their cocks in, but with the proper preparation, it is absolutely wonderful. Trust me, I know from experience."

I stored the information and decision for later. We returned to the main area and...surprising calm.

My bar remained intact, and my two men were sitting at the bar nonchalantly tossing back shots.

"Did you guys kill the vamp?" Regret clutched me at the thought of his demise.

Auric fixed me with bright green eyes. "No. We thrashed him and promised to kill him if he ever so much as looked at you again."

"I threatened to eat him actually," David added with a shrug. His bare chest drew my eyes, and a quick peek showed him wearing the emergency pair of jeans I kept behind the bar. Having a shifter boyfriend who acted as bouncer meant keeping stashes of clothing everywhere.

I shook my head at them both. "You can't

entirely blame him for what happened. My magic was at fault, too." I didn't mention the fact that the vamp had obviously gone easy on them. I didn't want to antagonize my lovers after all. But seriously, a creature who could take out twelve demons without breaking a sweat would have done a lot more damage if so inclined. I wonder if he'd held back knowing I'd be pissed if he hurt my men. Curse the spurt of warmth at the thought.

"Your magic isn't the only thing at fault. You should have told us," Auric added, standing to face me. I recognized the look in his eyes. The one that said I was in big trouble.

Yay for me.

In the space of a heartbeat, I found myself scooped up and exiting the bar. As I waved goodbye, I shouted instructions to my staff on the closing of the bar.

I twined my arms around Auric's neck. "So, baby, what's the punishment going to be this time? Spanking. Forced oral. Tease and denial." I rattled off several pleasurable ways he and David had punished me in the past, but he didn't reply.

Ooh, anticipation. I loved it.

Once he'd ascertained we were free from prying human eyes, Auric let his shadow wings come forth. "I'll meet you at the loft," he told David.

"I'll be ready," David replied with a grin before bursting free from yet another pair of jeans. The man and his kitty were truly hard on their wardrobe.

With a flap of his wings, Auric lifted from the ground, and I hung tight for the ride. I planned on easing my punishment with a bit of kissing and groping, but Auric wouldn't cave to my seduction.

"Why didn't you tell me what happened?"

Anger I could handle, threats and curses, too, but the quiet pain? It killed me. "I was afraid to hurt you," I whispered.

"Finding out from him hurt worse."

"I'm sorry. I know it doesn't make it better, but truly, I never meant for the kiss to happen, and once it did, I just wanted to protect you," I admitted.

"Did you enjoy it?"

Here came the squirming question. The truth or not? I looked up into Auric's green gaze and sighed. "I liked it. Or, more specifically, my magic did."

"Nefertiti warned me your magic would seek new sources to feed its different aspects."

His words took me off guard. "What? When did you speak to that old witch?" And more importantly, which version had he spoken to? The shriveled old prune or the naked, nubile nympho?

"You can get that jealous gleam out of your eyes and retract your claws," he replied with a chuckle.

I realized my fingers had dug into his skin, my nails digging into his flesh in my upset. "Explain."

"When we found out about your magic, knowing your propensity for not asking questions or getting information, I asked for you."

"And?"

"There are many facets to your magic. In order to access them all, you need specific types of lovers to feed them."

"Exactly how many types?" I whispered, suddenly appalled at the direction of this conversation.

"She wasn't sure. She knew of at least ten, but she said there could be more."

"Oh, fuck me." I leaned my head into Auric. I still had a hard time reconciling myself with the fact that I needed two lovers to sustain me. The thought of more appalled me.

"Before you get all freaked out, she did mention that, while your magic might be attracted to beings offering these other facets, it doesn't mean you need them."

I sensed a 'but' coming. "Don't stop now."

"So long as you keep your magic well fed, we can stop your magic from attempting to draw others to you."

"Let me get this straight. If my magic gets hungry, I'm going to be like some magnet for other beings who will feed my parasitic power?"

"Only if they fulfill a part of you that doesn't already have a connection."

My brain turned into mush as I tried to understand it all.

Auric took pity. "As an angel, even a fallen one, I feed your soul. David feeds your animal side."

"The vampire feeds the cold and dark," I continued.

"And if you found yourself powerless in the middle of the ocean, you'd draw a merman to feed the aquatic part of it. And so forth."

"Wait a second? Did you say merman? Does that mean there are mermaids, too?"

"Yes and yes. But don't get off topic. Do you understand what I'm saying?"

"If my batteries run low, my power is going to go hunting for the nearest being who satisfies a part of it and tie them to me, whether they want to or not."

Everything suddenly became crystal clear, and I didn't like it one bit.

Auric's eyes took on a resigned cast at my insightful assumption. "Yes. That's exactly it, but only if you're weak from power loss. We'll just have to make sure that never happens."

"It already has," I grumbled. "Or have you forgotten Fang Boy?"

Auric's lips tightened. "I'll need to confirm with Nefertiti if just a kiss can tie him to you or if it requires something deeper."

Given my reaction to his return at my bar, I already knew. Coitus might not have happened, yet my magic recognized the vamp as mine. And, even worse, the fact didn't bother me as much as it should have.

Auric had flown us through the night skies in loops while we had our talk. He landed on the fire escape and had no sooner set me on my feet than David opened the fire door.

"Is it ready?" Auric asked.

David nodded as he pulled me in to him for a kiss, distracting me from asking what the heck Auric was talking about. He walked me backward until my knees hit the bed, and then he turned me so I faced away from him. Auric came at me from across the bed in a predatory crawl that sent instant moist heat to my cleft. He stopped and knelt in front of me.

"Are you ready for your punishment?" Auric asked.

"I thought we'd talked that all out," I replied with a smile. Not that I wanted to get out of my punishment. Only an idiot would try to escape when I knew the pleasure that could be had.

"Our talk was important, but the fact remains that you hid something important from David and me. No secrets, baby. Rule number one and one I'll make sure you never forget."

The promise in his tone made my breath hitch. Auric smiled wickedly, his green eyes dancing. He nabbed me around the waist and leaned in for a kiss, more like a tease, as he only lightly brushed his over mine in a whispery caress that made me moan and lean in to him for more.

When I would have wrapped my arms around him, David grabbed my hands and pulled them up and out from me. Their mastery of me excited me, so I didn't immediately panic when the first manacle went around my wrist, followed by a second around my other. But I did worry when they both moved away and stopped touching me.

I opened my eyes and saw Auric leaning back

watching me. I licked my lips when he stripped off his shirt then his pants. David came into view and knelt up on the bed beside Auric, the pair of them naked, muscled gods, and even better, they belonged to me.

"I'm feeling a little overdressed here," I said, arching a brow.

"We wouldn't want that, given what we intend to do to you," Auric murmured. He leaned forward and used his bare hands to literally tear the clothes from my body.

I just about came, the evident strength and erotic appeal of the moment too much to bear. My naked skin shivered in the cooler air, and my nipples hardened into nubs. And still my boys watched me, raking me in with their heated gaze from head to toe.

"Feel free to start anytime." I would have taken matters into my own hands, but given they were shackled, I was completely at their mercy. My sex moistened further at that reminder.

"Impatient for your punishment?" Auric looked past me to David. "I'm surprised she's so eager for us to begin, given her vehemence over the whole ass issue."

I gaped and then screeched as understanding washed over me. "I don't think so. You can forget that plan right now. Spank me, bite me, or tease me, but you leave my ass alone."

David grinned. "You wish. Apparently you didn't get the memo about the fact we own your ass, so we're going to show you, in the flesh."

"But—"

"Your butt is ours," Auric interrupted. "And when something happens to it, you will let us know. I warned you this would be a lesson you wouldn't forget. Don't forget what I told you about your magic. If David and I don't feed it, your magic will find someone else who will."

I bit my lip to prevent the smile that threatened. I'd decided earlier during my talk with Bambi to let them have a go at my virgin hole, but letting them think they were in charge was so much more fun. I gave a resigned sigh. "Fine. Do your worst, but I'd better enjoy it."

"Oh, you will," Auric promised, stroking his cock, and now I felt fear. My consort's prick was not only long but thick, very freaking thick.

David chuckled when he caught the direction of my gaze. "Don't worry. He lost the coin toss for this first time."

Thank Hell. David, while lengthy, had a slender cock compared to Auric. I waited for them to start, but they lay back on the bed, stroking their cocks as they watched me dangle in my restraints.

I squirmed under their gazes, my nipples sharp enough to cut glass and my pussy so wet I expected it to start dripping. "What are you waiting for?" I asked, making a moue of impatience. The anticipation seemed likely to kill me.

"Beg for it."

"Lick me, kiss me, fuck me." I covered all my bases.

"Oh, we intend to. I want you to beg us to both take you. Beg David to take your ass while I take your pussy."

Okay, I think my eyes might have rolled back in my head for a minute, and I had a definite orgasmic quiver. Dirty talk tended to have that effect on me, and Auric knew it, the jerk.

"Fuck me." I wetted my lips. "I want you to fuck me in my tight virgin ass, David, while Auric fucks my wet and ready pussy."

That got them moving. In a flash Auric knelt before me, the head of his cock poking my lower belly. David moved to stand behind me, his hands on my ass cheeks massaging them. Caught between them, my desire raged out of control. The brushing of their skin against mine and the anticipation that hung in the air were potent aphrodisiacs, reminding me once again how truly lucky I was.

Auric caught my mouth with his while his fingers slid down my body to my sex. He stroked his digits across my wet cleft, using my own moisture to lube his fingers and rub my clit.

I moaned into his mouth, a sound repeated when David dropped to his knees at my rear and spread my cheeks to blow softly on me. I tried to squirm, to no avail, but I managed to clench my cheeks, again to no avail, as David used his strength to keep me open to his tongue laving me. Not to be outdone, Auric flattened himself on the bed on his back. He aligned his face with my sex and darted his tongue out to lap at me. Their dual oral probing and licking of my orifices had me twitching and gasping as I dangled from the restraints.

Exquisite torture. Their sensual attention wound me tight with pleasure. When Auric thrust a finger into my pussy as David penetrated my ass with a digit, I came with a yell, my channel quivering wetly.

But they weren't done. Auric returned to his kneeling position, and he kissed me, his mouth tasting of me, a strangely intimate thing. David stood behind me, his cock bobbing under me hotly, drenching itself in the moistness seeping from my sex. Auric's mouth left mine to latch onto a nipple. He sucked and tugged on it, his teeth nipping lightly, a shocking tease that sent zings down to my pussy.

David kept rubbing his hard cock against my wet slit while his finger circled my clit, teasing it by not touching it. I growled, as they didn't give me what I wanted. They laughed. Stupid, lovable jerks.

I squirmed as they both caressed me, ignoring my pants, paying no heed to my curses, reigniting my arousal until I pleaded, "Fuck me." I resorted to begging, "Please."

Auric grabbed hold of my waist with his large capable hands. He hoisted me, and I trembled at the feel of David's cock pressing against my back hole. The pressure as he stretched me made me try to squirm, but my men held me as David eased himself in, or attempted to. My juices dribbled on his rod, lubing his way. Personally, I didn't think it was going to fit, and I really wasn't sure I liked it.

"Relax," Auric murmured.

"You try to relax with a battering ram being shoved in your ass," I growled.

"Push out," David grunted.

I didn't understand what he meant. Wasn't trying to push him out counterproductive? But given the discomfort, I was game to putting a stop to it. I pushed out, and the bastard slid in. I yelped, my ass suddenly full of cock.

"Oh fuck," David groaned, not moving. "Hurry up, Auric. I am not going to last long."

I wanted to tell Auric to forget about shoving his fat cock into my pussy. Seriously, I had no room left, but he proved me wrong before I could open my mouth. Auric sheathed himself into me, and at the full sensation, I screamed, my channel clenching with spasms.

I kept yelling happy sounds as my men began to plow me, David in, Auric out, and vice versa. It blew me away how good it felt. How quickly and hard it ramped up my pleasure. Even more astonishing, my body rippled in orgasm and wouldn't stop.

Faster and faster, they plunged into me, losing their alternating rhythm to fuck me in cadence. My body tightened so rigidly I expected it shatter. As it was, I burst apart at the blissful seams as they thrust into me and filled me with their cocks and then with their essence. I saw stars, billions of them.

When I regained consciousness, I found myself on the bed, snuggled between them.

"Are you okay?" Auric asked, his voice laced with concern.

"Holy fuck," I managed to say, still overwhelmed. "Remind me to send you to Nefertiti more often for tips. That fucking rocked."

And it rocked again the second time, too, after our shower for foreplay, where they showed me a new oral technique. Lucky me.

CHAPTER FIVE

*T*he following morning found me sore, but not unpleasantly so. What do you know, I'd survived my first anal invasion—giggle—and I could grudgingly admit Nefertiti hadn't been kidding when she said the magic from a sandwich proved more potent. I fairly burst with power. Turn off the lights and I just might glow. As to the method involved in getting so magically full? Wickedly pleasurable.

Drinking a cup of coffee, decaffeinated because it was better for the baby—or so Auric informed me, the man having Googled the fuck out of pregnancy while I slept—I munched on my toast slathered in Nutella while reading the newspaper. Okay, I lied. I perused the latest copy of *Cosmopolitan*. An evil magazine, partly owned by my father. I loved to curse out the slim and smooth-skinned women who modeled for them.

My dad's cologne, Eau of Brimstone, wafted in as David answered a knock at our loft door. I almost fell off my chair in surprise. Had my father just shown us respect and employed some manners? I didn't think he knew how. Daddy usually preferred to just pop in and surprise the fuck out of us. Nothing shriveled a man's cock like having the devil say, "Nice white cheeks, boy."

But daddy dear hadn't waited for the most awkward moment to arrive. He'd knocked. Like a normal person.

"Don't tell me Hell froze over again," I said, shocked he'd actually come through the door.

"Nonsense. I'm just respecting your right to privacy like you asked."

I glared. "Who are you, and what have you done with my dad?"

My father chuckled. "Expect the unexpected. It's my new motto. And how's my darling daughter this morning?" He beamed as he presented me with a present he pulled out of thin air. It was all about showmanship, my father had once related to me. Having powers was fine and dandy. It was how you used them that impressed people.

I eyed the large package for only a second before tearing the pink paper and bow off to reveal a—I read the label—breast pump.

"What the heck is this for?" I exclaimed as I went cross-eyed looking at the medieval contraption that seemed to promise pain to my poor boobies.

"I've been reading up on the whole baby thing, and did you know, the doctors all seem to agree that breast feeding is the best form of nutrition for a baby. I thought a breast pump would be a way you could provide the best for the child while still maintaining some of your freedom." My father smiled even wider.

I choked, and Auric, his eyes suspiciously bright, hurried to rub my back while David turned around, his shoulders shaking suspiciously.

"You were reading up on babies?" I sputtered.

"Of course I was. Do you realize this will be my first non-demonic granddaughter?"

Hunh, that hadn't occurred to me. My succubi sisters tended to mate with demons because they had no souls. As for me, while I did have my daddy's eyes, the one thing all his evil scientists agreed on was that I wasn't a demon. Still, though, that wasn't the important thing at the moment. I gaped at my dad. "Holy fuck. You're actually excited about this whole pregnancy thing. Didn't Nefertiti tell you that my little bun in the oven might end the world?"

Dad shrugged. "A little apocalypse never caused permanent damage. Heck, my brother, God, threw a temper tantrum years ago and flooded the mortal plane. People called it the end of the world at the time, but what do you know, humanity made a comeback with the help of that Noah fellow."

I couldn't help myself. I laughed. "I love you, Dad."

My father, lord of the pit, scourge of mankind, squirmed, and while I couldn't be sure with his tanned complexion, I think he even blushed. "Yes, well, I'm fond of you, too. Just don't tell anyone."

How I loved these rare mushy moments where my dad, in his own perverse way, showed me his affection. "Don't worry, no one would believe me anyway," I replied with a smirk. "Any news on Azazel?" I asked before taking a big bite of the banana David placed in front of me. It seemed my men were determined to make sure I ate well, their way of showing support and love for me and our child. It was enough to make me gag, but I'd allow it for now. Besides, if they intended to keep feeding me, I'd enjoy it, so long as they didn't withhold the bacon. My appetite currently knew no bounds.

"My hunter found Azazel's tracks coming out of the Styx, but then lost them when they disappeared into the wilds of Hell. We're assembling some squads to go in after him."

"Maybe we'll get lucky and something will eat him," I grumbled.

"The spell of immortality has been pulled from him, so you may get your wish. On another note, your mother really wants to speak with you." My dad tossed that out there and then retreated behind the kitchen island. Ha, like that flimsy barrier would stop me if I got pissed.

I scowled. "Sure she wants to talk to me. I mean, she's so keen on reconnecting, that's why she hasn't called." And no, that ache in my heart had nothing to do with her lack of attempt to reconcile.

My dad grinned. "She's afraid you'll crawl through the phone to strangle her. You really made quite the impression on her."

I chortled. "Good."

"I think we should talk with her," Auric chimed in.

I glared daggers at him. "I have nothing to say to that woman." I lied. I had a zillion questions, but given my recent emotional stability, I doubted my ability to ask them and then receive the answers without turning into a blubbering mess. Given a choice, I'd take my usual psychotic self over emotional me any day.

My dad sighed. "That's what I thought you'd say, but I told Gaia I'd try. If you change your mind, here's her number."

He slid a great big green leaf over to me, and with a you've-got-to-be-kidding-me look, I took it. It seemed higher powers just couldn't do things in a normal fashion. Whatever happened to scribbling a real phone number on a napkin? I stored the leaf for later use—I never knew when we might run out of toilet paper.

I chatted with my dad as he outlined grandiose plans he had for creating a playroom in his castle for his granddaughter with all the best inventions a child could ask for. I did have to point out that it'd be a couple of years before she could play *Rock Band* with my dad and lovers. That didn't stop them at all from arguing over who got to be drummer. The whole thing touched me and threatened to draw more dreaded tears. Ugh, look at me turning into a ginormous pussy.

I wandered away from the good-natured arguing over to the bank of windows lining the wall. I stared unseeing outside, the cogs of the wheel in my mind turning and churning out a plan. The type of plan my consort and kitty cat wouldn't like at all.

A little voice in my head niggled me about the fact I'd promised Auric to not lie and come up with these brilliant ideas without involving him. However, some shames, such as why my own mother ditched me and refused to love me, were ones I wanted to deal with head-on—by myself.

Auric might not trust her, but she didn't scare me. It was probably dumb of me, but given my mother wanted the child I carried, I didn't think she'd hurt me, not until after the birth anyway. Then I'd wager all bets would be off.

"Don't you dare." Auric's voice so close to my ear made me shiver. Why was it I could never sense him approaching?

"What are you talking about?" I asked, a tad too brightly. I didn't turn to face him, certain my guilty thoughts would show in the color of my cheeks.

"Any idiot with half a brain can see the smoke coming from your ears as you think up some stupidly dangerous plot." His arms braced themselves on the windows, penning me in, not that I minded, especially when he pressed himself up against my back.

I sighed. "You know this whole soulmate thing sucks sometimes. Can't a girl have a secret?"

"Yes, my soulmate sucks and rather well, too. But let's not get off track. You plus a secret equals danger times a billion. So spill it before I cut you off from this." He grabbed my hand and placed it on his crotch.

I whirled and faced him with wide eyes. "You wouldn't dare. You know I need sex."

"And I need you to not go off half-cocked on some mad scheme that will get you in trouble. So I'm going to ask you one more time. Spill it."

"I'd rather not."

Green eyes narrowed. Lasered me with intensity.

Must fight it. Argh. It was impossible. Auric had my father beat when it came to giving 'the look'. I fidgeted, avoiding his gaze. I swear, for a fallen angel, he had some wicked mojo powers. One look in his eyes and I tended to promise things I had no intention of doing. Like doing the dishes and picking up after myself.

"Lucifer, I'm going to beat your daughter," Auric said in a tight voice.

"Go ahead. Stubborn chit never did listen to me."

"Daddy!" I couldn't believe my own father had thrown me under the bus, especially considering whom I'd inherited the pigheaded gene from.

"What? The boy has a point. You're stubborn. Don't know where you get that from."

The ginormous lie almost dragged a chuckle from me. I resisted and flicked a finger at my father, to no effect. My dad grinned at me, and I stuck out my tongue in a mature comeback.

As my lover crossed his arms, he continued to glare at me. With a sigh, I gave in. "Fine. I was thinking of going to see my mother."

Auric arched a brow. "Is it me, or didn't you, like just a minute ago, swear you wouldn't?"

"I'm a girl. It's my prerogative to change my mind as many times as I like." I smiled sweetly and batted my lashes.

"And I'm a man, so it's my right to say you are not going unless both David and I are with you."

"And me," my dad interjected. "Gaia is not as weak as you'd like to believe, Muriel. Some parts of my past with her are still fuzzy, but I do remember enough to know you don't want to cross her. She has a nasty temper. Just ask Pompeii."

My dad's statement distracted me from the men who needed lessons in the whole women-can-stand-on-their-own-two-feet situation. "Who the heck is Pompeii?"

"Not who, where. Forget it. The point is while I'm proud you've decided to face her and get some answers, the fact remains she's very dangerous, and you shouldn't go alone."

"Gee, Daddy, are you going to start holding my hand when I cross the road again, too?" My sarcastic comeback made David, who was watching the verbal sparring with interest, hide a grin behind his hand.

"I'm going to ground you if you keep lipping me, girl." My father's eyes began to burn in that special way only he and I could do. Like the coals of Hell, we were like freaking Rudolph with eyes instead of noses.

"If I were you, I'd stop pissing me off or I won't name the baby after you," I retorted.

I slapped a hand over my mouth as I slipped up on my surprise, too late. My father had heard, and the expression on his face was priceless. Actually, it kind of matched the look on my lovers' faces, too.

"Hey, don't look at me like that. Ever since I was a little girl, I've had the names of my children chosen. Lucinda Bambi for a girl and Lucifer Philokrates for a boy. Of course, now that I think of it, I guess you guys might want a say."

"I think Lucinda Bambi is a fine name," Auric said with a gentle smile.

David grinned. "I'm easy. Whatever makes you happy."

My dad, with suspiciously moist eyes, shoved Auric aside and hugged me tightly in an uncharacteristic gesture of affection. He whispered in my ear, low and probably spelled for my ears only. "I love you, Muriel. You do a father proud. But if you tell anyone, I'll cut your tongue out."

Smooch. I gave him a big, wet, loud kiss on the cheek in reply. My dad cleared his throat and moved away, trying to look gruff and commanding. I just thought he looked cute.

I clapped my hands and grinned. "Okay, now that we've gotten all stupidly sentimental and decided I'm taking a whole posse to visit Gaia, I need some food. I'm starved again."

"Let's go out for dinner," my father suggested.

"But the bar?" I protested only half-heartedly, already drooling at the thought of the things I could order and sink my teeth into.

"Your staff can handle the bar for one night," Auric replied.

"Besides, it's my treat," my father announced magnanimously.

My dad offering to pay for something? I clutched my heart. "Jeez, dad, are you trying to kill me today?"

"Smartass. Don't make me give you a zit on your nose."

To gales of laughter and more good-natured ribbing, we went to dinner, where I stuffed my face. Steak, potatoes, Caesar salad, garlic bread, part of Auric's lobster tail, several of David's shrimp. I would have tried some of my dad's chicken, but he threatened me with the tines of his fork, so I settled for two kinds of cheesecake for dessert.

I patted my satisfied belly after dinner and almost froze in horror. The bulge at my midsection was already becoming more distinct, bringing Nefertiti's words to mind. Perhaps I should plan to visit her again and ask how quickly this baby was coming. At the rate I seemed to be going, I'd probably see my tummy explode with Mini-me before the end of the month. Eek! That wasn't good. I hadn't even had a chance to go shopping for girl clothes yet.

The several glasses of water I drank with dinner made their presence known. I excused myself, but given my dad was there and hated manners, it was more along the lines of, "I've got to pee like a hellhorse." The napkin in my lap, which caught more than one drip, got tossed on the table before I headed to the ladies' washroom. The weight of Auric's gaze settled on my back. The only reason he didn't physically follow me was because he knew there were no windows in the bathroom and he could see the door from where he sat. Paranoia was his constant companion where I was concerned. Me, I had no fear. Public places crawling with humans were as safe as I could get. Besides, I had enough faith in my abilities to protect myself if the need arose and a wicked scream that would fetch my boys if the situation got sticky.

I pushed into the bathroom, which buzzed with feminine laughter as other diners refreshed their lipstick. Nothing tickled my senses as I moved farther into the washroom. A good thing because, had something jumped out and startled me, I might have peed my pants. I really had to go. I chose the farthermost stall, whose door hung ajar. I walked in and stopped dead at the unexpected sight.

And no, it wasn't a nasty unflushed toilet. It was worse.

I whirled, but the bathroom and its antiseptic smell had disappeared. Instead, I found myself in a lush garden overflowing with flowers.

What do you know? I guess I should have brought Auric along to wipe my ass after all.

I refused to allow myself to panic at my sudden interdimensional hop. Instead, with my head held high, I turned in a three-hundred-and-sixty-degree circle to take stock of my location. Seeing nothing, I took care of business first. I dropped my pants and did a weird squat with my ass hanging out. I tried not to whistle as I relieved myself. Done, I zipped up and moved away from the pond I'd created, congratulating myself on missing my feet. Aim was for boys. Girls just prayed they weren't on a slope.

Feeling better, I took stock of my location. Wherever I found myself, it sure appeared pretty. Lush plants grew all over the place, their vivid green foliage a beautiful counterpoint to the bright blooms flowering all over the place. Trees, majestic and tall, stretched up to a sky so blue I realized I hadn't just left Kansas; I was no longer in the good old United States of America. I could see no signs of life, nor hear any, not even the humming or buzz of insects. Eerie, kind of like when the power went out and the apartment went dead silent.

My body tense, I kept pivoting to see something, anything, in this garden that surely rivaled that of the legendary Eden.

And just that quickly, I knew who'd kidnapped me.

"Gaia," I spat.

"Won't you call me mother?" The petite form of the bitch who'd stolen me from under my lovers' and father's noses emerged from the jungle. Dressed like some kind of a wood nymph in a green gossamer gown with a crown of flowers, she would have appeared cute if not for the smirk on her face. A smirk I'd gladly wipe off.

"How about I call you dead meat?" I lunged at the cow, intending to show her what I thought about her little kidnapping stunt, but I hit a barrier and bounced back. I retained my balance, but my temper broke through my wall of cool. "You send me back right this instant. I'm the one who decides when and where we speak."

She tsked me. "Such a violent temper."

"You forgot to add in potty mouth, too, you irritating bitch."

A loud sigh left her. "I blame myself for how you turned out. I knew Luc wouldn't provide the most wholesome home for you to grow up in. But I didn't have much of a choice."

"Don't you criticize my dad. He was there for me. You weren't."

"But I'm trying to change that. It's why I arranged this meeting."

"Would it have killed you to perhaps call once or twice in my life to just say hi."

Even her snort sounded dainty. "As if you wouldn't have hung up."

Was it the mother-bond thing that already had her knowing me so well? "I would have eventually agreed to talk to you." Say when Hell froze over, again.

"I couldn't wait for you to put on your big girl panties. Given we only have a short time, I had to act, especially once I overheard your father and lovers planning to come along for the meeting. Men just get in the way. I thought we'd get more accomplished talking face to face. Mother to daughter. So calm down and act your age."

Talk about waving a red flag. I'd act whatever age I damned well pleased, and right now, the terrible twos with their inevitable tantrums really appealed. Common sense reared its head, which really surprised me. I didn't often hear from that particular facet of myself. It pointed out something interesting. Gaia currently held the upper hand, or thought she did. But mommy dearest had forgotten one thing— she wasn't the only one with power. After last night's orgy, I overflowed with it.

As often happened in a time of need, the ability

to use my power came naturally. I drew my magic around me and used it like a battering ram to charge through the force field she'd erected to stop me.

Her eyes opened wide in alarm as I stalked toward her with a nasty grin. "What do you think you're doing?"

"Reminding you that I grew up while you were gone. I'm not a defenseless little girl anymore."

She lifted her hands in surrender. "Would you stop it with the violent threats? I brought you here to talk."

"Great, because my fist wants really wants to say hello."

With more strength than I would have credited her, she caught my clenched hand before it could connect with her visage. Gaia gritted her teeth as she prevented it from landing, and I noticed a pearl of sweat roll down the side of her face.

"You're in danger," she gasped.

"Gee, I hadn't noticed. News flash. I've been in danger my entire life. Oh, that's right, you wouldn't know since you ditched me like yesterday's news." Bitterness colored my tone, and it annoyed me that I could still feel hurt over something that happened so long ago. I pushed harder to free my fist.

"I had to abandon you so you could fulfill your destiny."

"My destiny to what? Become a bartender?" I guess I'd failed in whatever destiny my mother had planned for me.

"No, to create the child who will save us all."

Her words froze me.

"Nefertiti says my child might end the world."

"That old hag thinks anyone with power will. But it doesn't have to be that way. Yes, your daughter will have great power. But it can be used for good."

Used. That word struck me. Everything from my mother's abandonment to her sudden return all seemed to revolve around one thing. "Why all this interest in my baby?"

"Stop trying to hurt me, and I'll tell you."

A part of me actually didn't want to know. Childish but true. However, it wasn't just about me anymore. I had a responsibility to my unborn child and lovers. Ugh, the responsible part of me wanted to gag.

"Before I let you go, answer one question. Did you ever regret having and ditching me?"

For the first time since I'd met her, my mother's face softened into a look that could almost be termed maternal. "I always wanted you, Muriel."

"Then why did you abandon me?" I heard the little girl plea, the weakness in my voice, and it disgusted me. Surely, I didn't care what she had to say.

"I had no choice. In order for you to fulfill your destiny, you needed to be strong. Know how to fight. I couldn't teach you that. Nor could I stand by and watch as you learned to be hard and merciless. You had a destiny to follow, one that would form you into the woman you are today and allow you to meet the men who would give you the treasure needed to stop the darkness from killing us all."

I let go of my mother and whirled to move away. I needed space. "You sent me to Hell."

"To a father who loved you."

"To fight for my right to live." My whole life, I'd battled to stay in the land of the living. Being a princess of Hell wasn't all about cool clothes and breaking laws, although those were definite perks. It also meant everyone wanted to use me or, if they couldn't use me, kill me for the glory.

"Your upbringing gave you the strength you needed and the ability to defend yourself."

"And how did growing up without a mother help me?" I threw at her and waited for her pitiful reasoning.

"It was a sacrifice that had to be made and one of my biggest regrets."

The shock of her admission jolted me, and I stumbled. I would have fallen, but a cushion of air caught me. I ended up sinking to the ground anyway, not trusting my legs, as all the emotional bombardments made me weak.

I drew my knees up and rested my face against them. In that moment, I wished that I had Auric by my side. He would not only hold me, safe and secure in his arms, he'd know if she spoke true because surely I read her wrong. Gaia sounded sincere, regretful, which went against everything I'd ever thought.

A hesitant touch stroked my hair. The only caress I'd ever received from my mother that I remembered. Tears pricked my eyes as my pregnancy hormones kicked in again when I least wanted them. "I don't understand anything anymore," I whispered.

"You've had a tough life, but I knew you could handle it. Those five years we spent together, marvelous years I might add, I did my best to teach you as much as I could in order to prepare you for the day I foresaw coming."

"I don't remember anything before I came to live with Dad."

"In order to protect you, I locked your memories away. Had that wicked angel, Gabriel, not messed with your mind, they would have been released at our first meeting. I know you can't remember, but you were happy with me."

I didn't reply, not trusting my voice not to break. However, time passed as I struggled to remember something lost in the labyrinth of my mind, enough time that Auric was probably freaking and David was hacking up hairballs at my disappearance. I needed to wrap things up so I could go home and mull over what I'd learned—a.k.a. have wild monkey sex to forget the emotional turmoil of the last few minutes.

I changed subjects. "Let's skip me for a minute and talk about the baby. I went to see Nefertiti. She says I should abort. That the child I carry is a threat."

My mother moved back from me, and I tilted my head to look at her. "She's correct in a sense. But then again, she said the same about you once upon a time. A person of power is only dangerous in the wrong hands. It's why you need to give your daughter to me."

My hair flew as I shook my head violently. "No!"

I set my chin to its most obstinate angle and glared at her. "Why should I give her to you? You couldn't handle me, so what makes you think you could deal with her? Besides, you said it yourself. I'm strong. Her fathers are strong. And she's got a grandpa who's someone to be reckoned with. Together, we can not only protect her we can also guide her along the right paths."

I expected her to freak out and start yelling, but instead, she inclined her head. "I'll grant you there's a possibility you would succeed. However, keep in mind, I've seen one of the futures, and in it, everything's gone. Heaven, Hell, Earth, wiped clean and all that is left is a gray nothingness."

"One future." I scoffed. "And how do you know that wasn't the one where you got your hands on the baby?"

"Because in one of the futures where I get my granddaughter, we prevail against the apocalypse and your child takes my place."

"And where are you?"

"Dead."

Yeah, that declaration kind of sucked the wind from my sails. "Seen any other possible futures you'd care to share?"

"Many, but most end in calamity."

Her words resonated inside me, like someone striking a gong right beside my eardrum, and the vibrations were so strong I could almost feel my teeth vibrate. I placed my hands over my rounded abdomen in a protective gesture. What she asked of me...it was too much. While I didn't doubt her good intentions and her belief, selfishness ran in my genes.

"I can't," I whispered. "I'm sorry, but unlike you, I don't have the strength to give away my child. Blame my father for that character trait if you will, but I won't sacrifice my child for the world."

"I hope you don't regret that choice."

At her words, I looked her straight in the face, our gazes locked in a silent struggle for power. "No. I'll never regret choosing my child. Unlike you, I believe things can turn out all right."

"So be it." My mother turned and walked away.

My jaw dropped. "Wait. Is that it? You're just going to leave?"

She paused and peered back over her shoulder. "You're not the woman I thought you were."

And with that verbal slap in the face, my mother left me—again. She took quick steps to the dense forest, which engulfed her, leaving me alone in a garden that no longer appeared so pretty to me. I suddenly regretted not killing her when I had the chance because I somehow knew this would come back to bite me. Not to mention her rejection of me for a second time in my life stung.

Tears blurred my vision as I sketched a portal to Hell, figuring that was where I'd find my dad and the boys who'd probably freaked when I didn't come back from the bathroom in the restaurant.

I stepped into the familiar heat and smell of Hell, but in an area I'd never visited before.

"What the fuck?" I exclaimed.

Figuring my pregnancy hormones had thrown my initial destination off, I attempted to draw another portal, but I never finished it. A sharp blow to the back of my head made me sink into darkness. And my last thought? Ha, Auric was wrong. My head's not that hard after all.

CHAPTER SIX

I should have gone with Muriel to the bathroom. It would have meant mockery from Lucifer, but Auric could have handled it, especially as it might have stopped the unease permeating him.

Despite how stalkerish it appeared, Auric couldn't stop himself from watching the bathroom door. No one entered other than Muriel, and he'd kept an eye on it even before that and with reason. His Google research into the whole pregnancy thing had made mention of the increased urge to urinate. Given Muriel had downed a few glasses of water with their meal, it was no surprise she had to go. And he let her without protest because, on top of his watching, he knew firsthand there was no other way into the washroom short of a portal, which Lucifer would sense in a second. It once might have irked him to rely on the devil for anything, but now he welcomed it. Lucifer might have a warped sense of values, but when it came to keeping Muriel safe, Auric knew he could count on him.

What of Muriel's own skills? Auric wasn't so chauvinist that he didn't recognize Muriel could take care of herself, but that didn't stop him from worrying.

A lot of people thought him overprotective of Muri, and he was, but with good reason, at least to him. He loved her. Truly loved her with every part of his being. David loved her, too, but unlike Auric, if Muriel were to exit his life, David would mourn then go on. If Muriel ever died on him, Auric would kill himself avenging her.

Before he'd met her, his life had consisted of one unending quest after another, meaningless events that ran together in his unwavering attempt to return to Heaven's graces. Then he'd met Muriel and found something better. He discovered a different kind of sunshine and perfection that made his previous life seem bleak.

His Muri could be crass at times, outspoken, and stubborn as a mule, but she also had a generous, loving heart and a courage that awed him. That fearless nature of hers, the confidence she could handle anyone and anything, while wonderful, scared the hell out of him. Muriel didn't know when to back down from a challenge, that and she tended toward impulsive action rather than carefully considered plans.

She kept putting herself in danger, and it terrified him. Not that he voiced that aloud. Auric had been raised in a time when males dominated women, and as an angel, with God's word as his guide, he'd chauvinistically used that to his advantage, believing in the doctrine that women belonged at home birthing and rearing the young. A thousand years of sexist ideology was a hard habit to break. Almost as hard as reminding himself that the older-looking gentleman sitting in front of him was supposed to be the scourge of mankind. The destroyer of souls. The lord of lies. His consort's father.

"Stop staring at the door. She isn't going to run away if you stop looking for a second."

"I'm not afraid of her running, Lucifer." Auric flicked his gaze over to his father-in-law and almost groaned as he saw the mischief lighting his expression. Much as he grumbled, Auric had, in the time since he'd gotten to know Lucifer, discovered a grudging fondness for the old devil, not that he'd ever admit that aloud.

"Haven't we gotten past first names yet? When are you gonna call me Dad? I mean you and Muri are living in sin, after all, and you've impregnated her out of wedlock. That makes you family, son."

Auric fought the urge to gnash his teeth at the deliberate baiting. While he'd begun to acquaint himself with Lucifer's odd quirks, his heavenly upbringing, so long entrenched, loved to rear its head. David saved him with his laughter.

"Oh, man, the look on your face right now, dude, is fucking priceless." David hooted as Auric glared at him, not amused in the least.

Rescue came from an unlikely source. "I wouldn't laugh so hard, furball. Him, I like, but you... Just because you're sleeping with my daughter doesn't mean you've passed in my books." Lucifer's toothy grin made David clamp his lips shut and gulp.

Auric's turn to chuckle.

Completely at ease, especially since he'd caused mischief, Lucifer sipped at his coffee. "So what's this I hear about you and the furball here attacking the hunter I sent to protect Muri?"

"What hunter?" Auric asked with a furrowed brow.

"The one I sent to the bar last night to meet Muri."

"Wait a second, are you talking about that vampire? The one who kissed Muriel?"

Lucifer's brows shot up, and his lips stretched into a thin line of displeasure. "Well. Well. It seems my spies have been lazy again. I'll have to take care of that right after I have a chat with my undead minion and make sure he understands that my daughter is no one's dinner."

"Glad we agree on something."

"We agree on more than you know, boy. Such as keeping Muri and that baby of hers safe."

"Safe from her mother you mean."

A grimace crossed Lucifer's face. "Much as it galls me to admit it, I don't think the woman means her harm. Gaia was always about the greater good and all that crap."

"You and Mother Nature..." Auric shook his head. "Talk about messed up."

"What is that supposed to mean?" Lucifer glared.

"Just that she's supposed to be all good and wholesome, and you're so...not."

A belly laughed escaped Lucifer as he leaned back in his chair, and Auric once again found his glance distracted by the yellow smiley faces on his tie, replete with a goatee and horns. The devil sure had his own sense of style.

"Gaia isn't a sweet and pure being. It's why she and my brother never went on more than a few dates."

"You stole God's girlfriend?"

Lucifer blinked. "Well, yeah. I mean, where do you think the whole sibling rivalry thing came from? Not that stealing her was hard to do, given I'm just so much more awesome and fun. You gotta admit, God can be a bit of a stick in the mud, which is funny given he hates dirt of all kind. He keeps the bleach and vacuum industry rolling in dough."

"So you dated Mother Earth?" David joined the conversation. "What was that like?"

Lucifer's eyes stared off into a past only he recalled, the most calming look Auric had ever seen crossed his face.

"It was the most wondrous thing. You have this perception of her as the mother of living things, the caretaker of this planet, but she is so much more. She is first and foremost a woman, with desires and a wicked sense of humor. She is passionate about so many things. I used to be one of them. Until the day she left."

Auric leaned forward. "Why did she leave? Did you know she was pregnant?"

"Know? I never even suspected. And then I forgot. We all did." Lucifer's brows beetled. "She took my memories from me. Stole my child for years."

"And then gave her back. Why?"

The query hung in the air because none of them had an answer.

Unease settled on Auric as the minutes ticked by and Muriel didn't reappear. He ignored David, who dodged Lucifer's verbal bombs and continued to watch the door to the women's washroom, willing it to open and spit Muriel out.

It remained shut as if determined to mock him, and the ball of unease grew. And exploded!

Auric sensed it the moment Muriel disappeared, as if someone had wrenched away a living, breathing part of himself and left a gaping, painful wound.

He stumbled from his chair, his usual grace lost in his fear. David and Lucifer both spoke to him, but he couldn't decipher their words through the white noise roaring in his head.

Without hesitation, he ran to the women's washroom and slammed through the swinging door, causing the females inside to squeal and berate him, with cries of "Pervert."

"Muriel!" he shouted, ignoring them. When she didn't reply, he did a quick search of the stalls. They all gaped at him emptily. Only in the last did he catch a whiff of her perfume, and there on the floor, he saw her purse. But no Muriel. Even worse, the part of his soul she'd claimed was gone.

Gone.

Auric fell to his knees under the weight of his grief. He opened his arms wide and screamed in primal rage. His beautiful Muriel was gone. Never to smile at him again. Never to tease him or stand up to him again. Auric wondered at the fact that Lucifer hadn't turned the world dark with his anguish, for much as the Lord of Hell would deny it if asked, he loved his daughter deeply.

And that simple thought pulled Auric from his self-inflicted misery. Why am I assuming she's dead? *Just because I can't feel my bond to her doesn't mean someone hasn't hidden her. After all, if anyone would know if she'd died, wouldn't her father?*

"Lucifer," Auric bellowed aloud, knowing the nosy devil would hear him.

He needn't have bothered because David and Lucifer had entered the bathroom behind him.

147

"Son, the next time you're going to invade the women's washroom and set them all screaming, give me some warning. That would have made an awesome HellTube video."

"This isn't the time for jokes. Muriel's gone."

"What? She left you?" Lucifer's face echoed his surprise.

"Gone, as in someone's taken her and hidden her. I can't feel her at all anymore."

David's face reflected the same shock as Auric felt. "My cat is freaking and telling me the same thing."

A negligent hand wave went with Lucifer's blasé "Maybe she's busy doing girly things. You know, snuck out of here because you were smothering her so she could baby stuff or something."

Auric resisted an urge to throttle the devil. "Muriel didn't fucking leave this bathroom through that door. She came in and never came out, so shut the fuck up and use your satany power or something and see if you can find her."

For a moment, Lucifer glared at him. "If you weren't her boyfriend..."

"But I am, and I'm telling you something is fucking wrong."

"I'm her father. If there was something wrong with Muri, I'd know it."

"Would you? You didn't even know who her mother was until a few days ago."

Lucifer's lips tightened. "I am really starting to dislike you, boy, and because of that, I will find her. Shopping. Or fornicating. Or starting a fucking war, and when I do, you will apologize to me, and I will lambast you with the biggest I told you so. And this is why men should never fall in love. It makes them weak."

"I'm not wrong." And his love didn't make him weak; it gave him meaning. Without it...

"Prepare to eat those words, boy." With a smirk on his lips, Lucifer concentrated.

It didn't take a magic user to feel the lord of the pit pulling at the esoteric waves that floated around. And then the devil didn't just pull. He yanked, harder and harder as his face turned red and his brows beetled together.

Steam began pouring from Lucifer's ears, and Auric winced when the devil let out a roar that shook the building and caused cracks to zigzag through the brick. "Someone stole my daughter!"

"Now do you believe me?" Auric asked dryly.

"I'll rip their intestines out and feed 'em to them. I'll flay their skin and roll them in salt. I'll—"

"Save your punishment for later. First, we need to find her. Find out if she's d-d—" Auric couldn't bring himself to say it.

"She's not dead," growled Lucifer. "I can still sense her spark, even if it's faint."

"Any idea where she is?" David asked as Auric searched within himself for a sign of his own that Muriel lived. All he found was a gaping hole where she belonged.

"She's in Hades."

Auric snorted. "Be a little more specific, would you? In case you hadn't noticed, Hell is pretty fucking vast."

"That's just it. Whatever is cloaking her is doing a pretty fine fucking job. All I know is she's somewhere in Hell, and not in any of the civilized parts."

Auric frowned at Lucifer. "Wait a second. You're Satan. How can you not know every inch of Hell?"

Lucifer shrugged. "The pit is always growing. It has to or we'd run out of room in no time, given the way the population on Earth keeps growing and with the numbers of people getting recycled in the abyss getting smaller all the time."

"So, she's in one of the newer sections then?"

"I don't know if I'd call it new. More like undiscovered and wild, really, really wild. It's not a place you want to go hunting in lightly."

Auric's heart tightened, his fear for her turning that muscle into a hard lump. "I don't have a choice. If Muriel's been captured, I need to go find her."

"Considering who I am, I really wish you'd cut out the altruistic stuff. It hurts my head, but at the same time, as her father, I have to say, much as it galls me, thank you."

The men looked at each other and glanced away, both uncomfortable.

David cleared the silence. "Okay, so we arm ourselves and go after her. Dangerous or not, we obviously can't sit back and wait for the perpetrator's next move."

"You can't just go running off into the wilds. You'd die the first day out."

"We're not sitting here on our asses waiting to see the kidnapper's next move," Auric growled.

"Never said you should, but if you want to survive, you need to take Teivel with you. He's the best tracker I've got, and he just might keep your sorry asses alive. Not that I care or anything, but Muriel is likely to throw a tantrum when she gets back if she finds out I let you get hurt."

Pride made Auric want to say he could do it on his own, but only an idiot would turn down help when the woman he loved faced danger. "Fine. David and I will need to gather some supplies. We'll meet you at the palace in an hour."

With a swirl of brimstone smoke, Lucifer disappeared, and not wanting to waste time, Auric drew a portal to the loft and stepped through with David.

David grabbed his arm. "Is Muriel going to be okay? My fucking kitty is freaking in my head. It's acting like she died or something."

David's admission surprised him. Auric had known David cared for Muriel, but his words implied something deeper. More permanent.

"Is she your mate?" Auric asked. He'd heard of fabled mating bond that occurred with shifters. Apparently, there was one perfect person to whom they could attach themselves. At his friend's nod, Auric realized that, while he might care deeply for Muriel, David had just as much at stake as he did. Mated shifters couldn't survive the death of their other half, or so legend claimed.

Grief was a powerful emotion, as was fear. Auric wanted to reassure his friend that they would find Muriel, but it shamed him to admit he felt doubt. "I pray we find her in time, but one way or another, whoever took her is about to get their head torn off and shoved up their ass for daring to lay a hand on her."

David returned Auric's cold smile with a frigid one of his own. "The bastard chose the wrong dudes to fuck with."

Wrong dudes indeed. *Hold on, baby, we're coming for you.*

CHAPTER SEVEN

*P*acking a bag didn't take long. When going on a mission, a man took only the essentials. Spare set of clothes, a sleeping bag, dried rations, a butane lighter, and a big fucking sword. Or, in David's case, a machete since he tended to fight in feline form, unlike Auric who liked to chop bad things to bits.

Once they were as prepared as they could be for the surprises the wilds of Hell would hold, Auric called a portal to Hell, a magical ability given to him by Lucifer. The movies claimed human summoners could open doors to Hell. Not really. Only the strongest demons and magic users with a certain type of power could do it or, as in Auric's case, those granted permission. Opening his own portal sure beat the old-fashioned method of finding a guarded gateway to Hades and then bargaining with Charon or his lackeys to cross the Styx.

As he and David stepped through the interdimensional rift, he inhaled the acrid and dry air of Hell, the soft sift of ash falling from the sky featherlight on his skin, but not oily or as dirty as it sounded. The ash was just a part of this landscape, a landscape that never ceased to surprise him. Having been created by God, for a long time he'd known only the purity and light of Heaven.

But Auric had one failing, many if you asked those who accused him. He wasn't content to sit around in the quiet and peace of Heaven. He wanted to swoop upon the earth and help those in need. Fight the forces of darkness. Make a difference.

Yeah, that kind of thinking had him cast out. But, in retrospect, it was probably the best thing to ever happen to him. Being forsaken meant he could do the things he'd yearned to for so long. He could change the world.

He could also, and did, fall in love. *I fell in love with Lucifer's daughter.* And because of their relationship, he'd gotten to know more than he could have imagined about Hell.

Stories spanning the centuries, and more

recently movies, portrayed Hell as some kind of burning inferno. Ask someone what the pit looked like and they'd almost unanimously say red rocks, deep crevices, molten lava, ugly demons with horns and tails, and let us not forget the damned, tortured for all eternity.

The reality didn't even come close.

In truth, Hell was very much like the human plane in the sense that the damned lived and worked here. They had families, just not new additions. But have a few generations die, and suddenly the place was crowded with relatives.

Geography wise, Hell was divided into rings, nine to be exact, and those rings were always stretching to accommodate the constant population growth. Winding through the rings was the Styx, a sinuous serpent of water, a deadly river full of monsters and considered impassable unless navigated by Charon and his fleet of ferrymen.

There was also a sea the Styx spilled into that kissed the shore of the ninth ring as well, the Darkling Sea, although where it went none had ever returned to tell the tale. The parts of the outer ring not bordered by water were known as the wilds. How long those stretched was anyone's guess. Those who managed to survive spoke of a never-ending forest, a vast jungle rife with pitfalls and savage beasts.

That was where Auric and David would have to go to search for Muriel, an impossible task, and yet, Auric would go on this quest. He would look forever if he had to in order to find the woman he loved.

These thoughts served to keep his mind occupied as he strode the dusty, cobbled road that led to Lucifer's castle. Nestled in the heart of the first ring, the stone block monstrosity loomed behind the highest rusted gates in existence, their ominous creak a cultivated sound effect meant to strike fear. Such parlor tricks didn't impress Auric, and David had visited one too many times to pay it any mind.

The major domo, a squat Atlantian, greeted them. For once, he appeared frazzled, his eyes more bloodshot than usual. Muriel was well loved by those who knew her. "You will find the princess," Phil stated.

"I won't stop searching until I do."

With a bob of his head, Phil ushered them into Lucifer's presence, the big man seated in his chair, barking on his phone. Against the fireplace, big enough to roast a few beasts whole, lounged a familiar vampire.

"If it isn't the angel and his pussy. I'd say it was

nice to see you again, yet given your countenance, I get the impression we are not of like mind."

"What are you doing here?" Auric snarled.

The vampire tossed him a grin. "I am here to help. I hear you need a guide."

"Like fuck am I going anywhere with you."

"Such foul language, I love it." Lucifer slammed his fist on his desk and beamed. "I can't wait to hear what happens on your trip."

"You're going to wait a long time because I'm not going anywhere with this womanizing freak. Find us someone else to use as a guide."

"Not going to happen, boy." Leaning back in his chair, behind a massive desk carved out of bone, Lucifer folded his hands over his chest. "Teivel's the best I've got."

"I don't give a damn. I want someone else," Auric growled. Once upon a time, he'd been a man who didn't understand jealousy. He coveted nothing. And then Muriel came into his life. He'd thought he'd lose his mind when he found out the only way to cure the nightmares and fear geas set on her meant inviting another man into their bed. But he'd gotten through it by ensuring that other man was David. If he had to share Muriel with anyone at all, let it be the man he loved like a brother.

Understanding Muriel's magic, and its insatiable need, though, didn't mean he would readily accept this undead hunter as well. He'd discovered that jealousy wasn't the only sin he was capable of. Greed was, too. Auric didn't want to share, not Muriel, not her heart, and most especially not the glory of finding her. He wanted her thanks for him and him alone.

And he didn't have it in him to feel shame at the realization.

Good thing David was a better man than him. His friend put a hand on his arm and spoke in a low murmur. "Like the guy or not, we need his skills. We need him to find Muriel."

The cool logic didn't completely sway Auric. He still wanted to refuse the vampire's aid, but his pride and prejudice weren't worth Muriel's life. "Fine. We'll work with the undead bastard, but I'm going on the record right now and stating that, if he attempts to feed off me, you, or anyone else, I'm staking his ass.

The dark-haired vampire snorted. "Afford me some credit, fallen one. As if I'd stoop to eating your sanctimonious ass. Although your blond kitty there would probably make a good meal."

Now it was Auric's turn to hold David back as he gnashed his teeth, his panther close to the surface.

"Enough!" Lucifer's voice boomed, the acoustics in this room taking it and echoing it. Given the menace in the single word, they all fell silent.

"Excellent. You're all still here. I was worried I'd be late."

At the dulcetly uttered words, masculine eyes whirled to see Gaia's petite form come striding into Lucifer's office, looking fetching in a pale green summer frock, dangling a straw bonnet from her hand.

"Who let you in?" Lucifer sputtered. Auric could understand his consternation, given the lord of the pit had spells preventing the opening of portals in the palace or within close proximity of it.

She adopted an innocent mien. "Since when is your wife not allowed in her own home?"

"Wife?" Lucifer's eyes bugged out of his face, and the way his face turned red made Auric wonder if he needed to worry about the old devil suffering a heart attack.

"Now, Luc, I realize you were drunk when we said our vows, but still, surely you remember our wedding night. We did, after all, conceive Muriel that night."

"I am not married. I am the father of sin. I would

never do something so gross as tie myself to one woman."

"You did. But never fear, I had it annulled when I realized I'd have to leave you. But still, as your ex-wife, I have rights."

"You have the right to march your sexy little ass back out those doors. You weren't invited."

"And here I thought you'd be so pleased I was flouting your desires."

"I'll tell you what I desire," Lucifer grumbled.

"Luc, please, not in front of the children." And then Mother Nature winked, which totally threw the devil for a jaw-dropping loop.

Auric took pity on his father-in-law. "What are you doing here, Gaia?"

Suddenly, she didn't look so cocky. "Well, I feel kind of responsible for Muriel disappearing, seeing as how it happened right after our little talk."

In that moment, with those words, Auric now understood Muriel's desire to throttle her mother. Auric barreled toward her, along with a transformed David and a bellowing Satan, but none of them could beat the vampire. Teivel reached Gaia first. His pale hand gripped her by the throat, and he held her aloft, ignoring the feet kicking.

"Where is she?" the vamp asked coldly. "What have you done to her?"

"While I approve of your methods," Auric stated as he skidded to a halt alongside the vampire, "she does need air to speak." A pity.

"Good point." Teivel loosened his grip, dropped her in a heap, and stood glaring at her, arms crossed across his chest.

While most people would have landed hard and ungainly, Gaia fluttered down in a cloud of filmy fabric, managing to look graceful and dainty.

It was disconcerting to watch because while, in some respects, Muriel resembled the woman, his lover possessed a lethal, not delicate, grace.

"That was rude." Gaia sat on the floor, rubbing her throat, her eyes watching them all warily.

"If you wanted manners, then you came to the wrong place," Lucifer stated. "You can't expect to waltz in here and admit to kidnapping Muriel without consequences."

"I didn't kidnap her."

"Lie!"

"Okay, I did, but only for a few minutes that we might chat. Last I saw her, she was fine."

"And where was that?" Auric asked.

"My garden. It was the only place I could think

of where we could talk uninterrupted." She dared to fix them with an indignant gaze.

"You kidnapped her so you could talk to her. And then what, imprisoned her until you could steal our child?" Auric's words were punctuated by a feline growl. David paced in front of her, hackles raised, lip peeled back in a snarl.

"Hold on a second. I did nothing to her. We just talked," Gaia protested. "When we were done, I left. From what the trees told me, she called a portal to Hell, only it went to the wilds, and then she disappeared."

An invisible force picked Gaia up and slammed her against the stone wall. Lucifer stalked forward and gone was the joking and cynical man Auric had gotten to know. Here was the devil, and his eyes glowed with the flames of the pit. His face rivaled that of a thundercloud.

A tremble of awe went through Auric at the power emanating from the usually affable Lucifer. Finally, they all got to see the true King of Hades, and Auric found himself glad he wasn't the one facing his wrath.

"You conniving little bitch. How dare you return after all this time and dick us around? Screw with my daughter. Muriel was right. We should have killed you."

"I swear. I had nothing to do with her current disappearance. I'm as mystified and as upset as you are."

Unfortunately, even Auric could tell that this time she appeared to tell the truth.

"Woman, you had better not be lying. I won't hesitate to punish you if you've done anything to harm our daughter and grandchild."

"Luc, I swear. I didn't mean her harm. I don't know how her portal out of my garden messed up. That was the work of another."

Lucifer stared at her a moment longer and then let the power that held her pinned like a bug on the wall dissolve.

He turned his back on her and thus missed the hand she stretched out to him and then snatched back. She straightened herself and strode over to the wall of maps. She perused them for a moment before stabbing her finger at a blank section. "Here. This is where the portal opened and dumped her."

Lucifer frowned at her. "How can you know that?"

"I'm Mother Earth. I know lots of things."

"That's not an answer. Even I can't pinpoint locations in the wild."

Gaia smirked. "Still relying on brute force I see. If you'd learn to control yourself, you'd be able to fine-tune your abilities."

"Oh, you're one to talk about control. What about all those tsunamis and tropical storms you've been brewing the last few years?"

"What? A woman can't have a bit of fun? You're one to talk with your public hangings and lashings."

"Someone has to keep order in the pit or the damned would run wild."

Putting two fingers in his mouth, Auric let out a strident whistle. "If you two are done comparing your deeds, can we get back to Muriel here? Now that we have a location, we'll just open a portal and go after her."

Teivel clucked his tongue. "Greenie. If it were that easy, do you think they'd be called the wilds?"

Frustration made Auric redden. "Fine then, what do you suggest we do?"

"Oh, we'll take a portal there, but I guarantee she's long gone. The best we can hope for is a clue as to her next destination." Teivel turned to Lucifer. "My Lord, if you could open a portal with the lady's coordinates."

Lucifer nodded, but before he could open it, Gaia grabbed his hand. At his startled look, she replied, "I'll help you pinpoint the location." A moment later, the portal, an inky maelstrom of darkness, appeared. Teivel, with a nod to Lucifer, dove through, followed by David still in kitty form.

Auric snagged David's pack and slung it over his shoulder, along with his own. Before he could step through, he found himself grabbed by Gaia.

"Find her," she whispered. "Or all will be lost."

"Kill them all," Lucifer spat. "Painfully."

Auric gave them a nod and strode through the portal.

Hold on, baby. I'm coming for you.

CHAPTER EIGHT

*S*mells good.

David's tail swished as he peered around cautiously at the jungle the portal had dumped them in. In his panther form, he could see and hear more clearly, not exactly an enjoyable thing in this place when wearing his human form, but as his kitty, fascinating. If the name Hell weren't already taken, it would have aptly described this nightmare. Where the jungles of Earth were lush, green places full of life, in Hades, their form was the antithesis.

Twisted and gnarled trees sprouted all over the place, their moldy foliage a mixture of reds and browns with black pulsing growths. The bushes and underbrush sported thorns that glistened wetly, and as he learned when he moved too close, they could move like a living entity. Paranoia wasn't the reason David could have sworn the bushes and trees watched them hungrily. It seemed, everywhere he looked, things lurked waiting for a misstep.

The one thing absent in this Satan-forsaken place was insect life. Usually in a jungle-like place, the buzz of mosquitoes would drive a person nuts, but here, their absence seemed conspicuous, as did the lack of spider webs.

Teivel, whose smell didn't so much remind David of a dead thing but of the cold, something he never knew had scent, took a machete out and hacked a few creeping vines, which caused the rest to retract with a hiss.

David saw Auric step through the portal a moment before it closed, and he padded over to his friend and butted his head against him. In this place of madness, he needed to reaffirm their solidarity. Auric rubbed his head before crouching in front of him.

"I'm here, buddy. Any sign of Muri?"

Chagrined, he'd not looked for a sign yet, too caught up in his examination of his surroundings, David sniffed the air and sifted the scents. He almost went cross-eyed as too many potent odors hit him at once. He took a moment to sort them. Foliage, brimstone, different foliage, some kind of animal with a musty scent, demon...a familiar demon.

David followed that trace scent and soon found another, a sweet, soft scent he knew so well. He walked forward to a flattened area of the bristly grass. A redness glistened wetly on the ground. It didn't take a sniff to recognize blood.

Teivel knelt a moment later by his side and touched a finger to the red stain. "She was here. Someone struck her down with this rock." Teivel held up a striated stone that bore more blood and also a few strands of dark hair.

It was encouraging that whoever had attacked had done so with such a crude weapon. Even better, the stains on the rock and ground weren't enough to have killed her.

Whoever had attacked wanted Muriel alive.

But who was it? In his feline shape, speaking wasn't happening, so David chuffed and looked pointedly at Teivel. *Come on, dude, smell the rock.*

"Patience, kitty. I was getting to it," Teivel said. He held the stone close to his nose. The vampire inhaled deeply and then growled. "Azazel. That old bastard."

"Are you certain?"

Teivel shot Auric a dark look. "Of course I'm

sure. That demon is the reason I ended up hunting in the wild."

"I should have fucking listened to Muriel," Auric growled. Teivel gave him a questioning look. "She has this theory that bad guys should always be killed on the spot instead of saving it for later."

A grin lightened the brooding vampire's countenance. "I am liking this girl more and more."

David and Auric both growled, which made Teivel laugh. "Holy fuck. Jealous much? Don't tell me you're afraid of a little competition?"

"We don't fear you. Muriel loves us."

"If you say so," the vampire taunted. He strode toward the jungle, hacking at the brave branches and vines that inched toward him. He paused in his whacking to peek back at them. "Are you coming, or am I rescuing her alone?"

"We're coming, Fangboy."

"That's Fangman. I am, after all, the eldest here, fallen one."

"And the most annoying," Auric muttered under his breath. "Where are we heading?" Auric hefted the packs higher on his shoulders whilst keeping a hand on the hilt of his sword.

"I forget, your type doesn't have a very good sense of smell," mocked the vampire. "For a race that considers itself better than others, you're not so well endowed." The implication didn't need the downward glance and smirk. "They took her this way."

Good thing David wore his cat or he would have laughed at the look on Auric's face. He loved his friend, but it was fun sometimes to see his dominant and overbearing friend meet someone who didn't bow to his presence.

And Teivel was right. The scent was obvious to those with refined olfactory senses and easy to follow. He padded after the vampire.

With a grumble about know-it-all vampires and stupid jungles that should be mowed down, Auric joined them.

Paying no heed to the noise he made because, as Teivel explained, "They already know we're here." The vamp slashed and hacked a path through the living forest. This perversion of nature that David didn't like at all. The farther they went, the more David prayed they'd find Muriel quickly and leave this forsaken place. The trees towered over them, blocking out the reddish glare that lit the planes of Hell, creating ominous shadows.

Did something lurk under that bush?

Was that dark shape something to watch for?

They'd walked for a while before the unnatural silence struck him.

The jungle around them appeared too still. David didn't trust it and took his cue from the vampire who, unlike earlier, moved with quiet steps. Teivel's head kept turning, as if searching the numerous shadowy pockets bracketing them. Signs of arachnids appeared, not that David found himself reassured at this sign of normal bug life, given the size of the webs he saw spun between the trees could have caught an elephant. Somehow, he doubted he'd want to meet the spinners of the webs in person. A futile hope.

"Watch out above you." Teivel shouted the warning, and just in time, too.

Arachnids dropped from the canopy of the trees. Actually, more like abominations, David noted with a shudder—a cross between spiders, appalling enough, and humans, or their heads at least.

One dog-sized creature landed on David's back, and he bucked, sending the creature flying, only to watch in horror as it scuttled back at him, its humanoid features horrifying, especially its dark orbs, the pupils a flat black that reflected nothing.

The thing's mouth opened wide, flashing two

rows of pointed teeth. It let out a screech that made his ears ring, a noise meant to intimidate.

Good luck with that. David wasn't a rookie to battle. That half-second pause let him assess his prey before he pounced on it and sank his fangs into its neck, ripping the offending head free. One down, dozens to go.

David tore into the disgusting creatures, their ichor spraying him as he ripped at their limbs using his teeth and claws. The acrid taste made him gag, which said a lot, given his cat usually wasn't too finicky about the flesh it ate.

A flash of silver light from behind meant Auric wielded his holy sword to deadly effect while, in front of him, with a blur of motion, Teivel dispatched the eight-legged monsters without breaking a sweat.

Dude had some seriously impressive moves.

As quickly as it had begun, they killed all the monstrous spiders. Teivel wiped his pair of daggers using a rag he'd pulled out. "Well, that was fun, if messy."

"Was it me, or did it seem like that attack was orchestrated?" Auric asked as he sheathed his gleaming blade.

"Probably, given these creatures never work in

groups." Teivel's expression had returned to its dark, grim one.

The fact that they thought the attack was planned made David wonder. He pawed at one of the freaky heads and chuffed in question.

"Looks like your kitty is curious. If I grasp what you're asking, then, no, these things aren't natural. The mutations began years ago, well before your birth. It's why Lucifer sent me into the wilds. He hoped I'd find the cause. I've brought back a few of the abominations, and according to Nefertiti, someone grafted a damned soul onto a regular wild spider."

"You mean someone is experimenting?" Auric's incredulous tone matched David's inner horror.

"More than experimenting now. Building a mutant army and using them to attack. If I were to wager a guess, I'd say whoever's been fucking with the wildlife is the one who's taken Muriel."

The vamp's words made David's stomach sink as the implication sank in.

Auric caught it, too. "The One. The bastard who's been fucking with Muriel and Lucifer. He's the one screwing with shit, and he's been under our noses this whole time."

"It's the conclusion my Lord came to recently as

well when I returned. Not that this helps us in our quest."

No, it doesn't, thought David. *But regardless of the odds, I won't give up. I can't. I know Auric thinks he loves Muriel more deeply than I. Perhaps he does, but regardless, I need Muriel. She is my mate, the mother of my child. The woman I love.*

No matter the odds, even if he had to forfeit his life, he'd not rest until he'd saved her. Or died trying.

CHAPTER NINE

*T*he pain in my head nagged at me. A headache of gigantic proportions threatened to burst free from my skull. Funny, because I didn't remember getting wasted.

"Auric," I moaned. "I need some Tylenol."

But it wasn't Auric who answered me.

"About time you woke up."

There was something about hearing the voice of a demon that I knew hated me that made my pounding head pale in comparison. My eyes shot open, and a few things struck me at once.

One, I had no idea where the fuck I was. Two, Azazel had definitely spoken. And three, according to my rumbling tummy, I was really freaking hungry again, but before I could feed myself, I had a teensy, tiny demon problem to deal with.

"Fancy running into you." I spoke nonchalantly, even as an inner part of me screamed. See, I'd just discovered a fourth thing. Straps held me immobile on some kind of gurney while IVs fed fluid into my arms. And we wouldn't focus on fact five, which was that I'd embraced unconsciousness long enough for my stomach to turn into a small hill.

Why do I get the feeling I'm in really big doo-doo?

Azazel's ugly mug came into view as he stepped to the foot of the hospital bed. "It would be in your best interest to play nice with me, Muriel. The One has promised you to me after the baby comes."

Panic clawed at me. I bitch slapped it and pasted a saucy grin on my face. "Like you'll live that long. Auric and David will find me, and when they do, I look forward to seeing them force you to eat your intestines." Actually, I'd probably gag if I had to watch, but I liked to paint an eloquent picture.

Azazel's squashed nose—squashed because it had been broken one too many times, and not just by me—flared, and his eyes glowed menacingly. "Why you little—"

"Leave." The single word spoken in a cold tone worked like a charm. Azazel turned like a puppet on strings and marched out.

A dumb person might have wondered who had

the power, other than my mom or dad, to order a high-level demon around. I didn't. There was only one being with that kind of the power. The one Gabriel called master.

With a patience I hated, but faked, I waited to see the person who'd fucked so much with my life lately. The one who kept screwing up my plans for a happily ever after. The one who wanted me—and my baby.

A figure draped in a silken, hooded robe drifted into view, the grey of the fabric a shimmering opalescent silk of the finest weave. I coveted the fabric, but I mocked the outfit.

"Good grief, get a sense of style. I mean, seriously, did you and Gabriel use the same tailor? Robes are so out. Get with the times. And what is it with you folks hiding your faces all the time? Have some pride, show your face." Because I really hated not seeing the visage of the person whose ass I was going to kick later. I wouldn't want to make a mistake, after all, when meting out punishment.

Fuck with me, will you? Not for long. I rocked at revenge, just ask headless Gabriel. Oops, you couldn't because I killed him.

Just like I'd kill...what hid under that robe anyhow? Were they distantly related to Charon?

The chuckle of the cloaked one chilled me, as did the slender hands that emerged from the sleeves to push back the hood to reveal... a woman? And a rather boring one at that.

Talk about a letdown. Whatever happened to really cool-looking bad guys, er girls? I mean, seriously, couldn't they make an effort to look intimidating, maybe add some horns, resort to eyeless sockets? Ooh, how about some saber-toothed fangs?

But no, my nemesis was a plain Jane. An unknown one at that.

I stared blankly at her, trying to figure out just who had captured me. I catalogued her appearance, tall, slender, with shoulder-length, jet-black hair, dark eyes, thin lips, and a look that said I've-got-the-biggest-stick-ever-up-my-ass. Nothing rang a bell. "Who are you?"

A perfectly manicured brow arched, and those bloodless lips curved into a smile I'm sure would have suited a lion just before it ate its prey. "I am Lilith."

She announced this as if I should know her. Apparently she needed a better PR team. "Never heard of you." I shrugged. She wouldn't be the first psycho to think the world should know her name.

"I am Lilith." I yawned. "From the Bible."

My blank stare didn't change. "The Bible? Yeah, sorry, but my dad doesn't like me reading stuff like that." He was still pissed my uncle had his ghost-writers picture him in such a bad light. Never mind the fact it was mostly accurate.

"I am Lilith, as in the woman thrown from the Garden of Eden. Lilith, as in Adam's lover," she said through gritted teeth.

The light bulb went off. "Oh, you're that crazy lady who pissed off Uncle God and ate that fruit thingy from his tree." At her glowering expression, it occurred to me I should have omitted the crazy part. Then again, I didn't plan to stay long, or let her live. "I heard about you. If I remember correctly, you ended up getting replaced by Eve as the mother of humanity and tossed out of the garden. Wow, I'll bet you regret that one, seeing as how Eve ended up getting all the glory." I smiled as I said this, quite enjoying the way her face turned beet red.

Just call me a bringer of joy, spreading happy barbs everywhere I go. Fun aside, now that I'd returned to the land of the conscious, the time had arrived for me to escape and find my family. I tugged on my magic. It didn't budge. Frowning, I pulled at it again. Again, nada. I didn't understand it. I could sense it in me, depleted, but still there.

Lilith cackled. "You didn't really think I'd leave you access to your magic, did you? I'd have drained it all away except the baby needs it."

Those words at least explained the tubes and shit sticking in my arms. The crazy lady wanted to keep me and the baby healthy.

"Just how long do you figure you can keep me here? You know my men are looking for me. They won't rest until I'm found."

"Oh, they're looking, but don't worry, I'm keeping them distracted with plenty of surprises."

That worried me a little, but knowing Auric, David, and my dad, they'd prevail, even if I couldn't be with them protecting their asses. "You are living on borrowed time, lady."

"Lilith."

"Whatever. Given how long it looks like I've been here, I'll bet they'll arrive anytime now and kick your scrawny ass."

Again, she graced me with the smirk I really hated. "I hate to break it you, Satan's spawn, but what seems like only days to them has, in actuality, been weeks for you. Congrats, it won't be long now before the babe is born."

Why did the bad guys always have the better magic? "You won't get away with this."

"I already have."

"You leave my baby alone," I shouted.

"Sorry, but that daughter you carry will be mine."

This running theme of taking my baby away really grated on my last nerve. "I'm going to tear your head off and use it as fish bait. I'm going to submerge you slowly in acid. I'm—"

"Going to sleep," she announced before injecting me with a needle and depressing the plunger.

Instant fatigue invaded my system, and as I fought the blackness, I sent a mental scream.

Auric, save me!

CHAPTER TEN

*A*uric lost track of how long they'd marched through the wilds. More than a day, less than a week. Long, sweaty, tiring hours filled with attacks from creatures that belonged only in horror flicks and Wes Craven's sick mind.

In that time, he'd come to grudgingly respect the vampire who'd saved David's and his lives countless times, especially since Auric knew Teivel hungered after their last attack, and yet, not once had he asked or implied that they should feed him. Which was why, when they camped that night, Auric thrust his arm at the vamp and said, "Eat. You need your strength."

"I prefer a more feminine meal."

"Do you see any women here?" No need to look around. Auric shook his arm at the vamp again.

"Don't be an idiot. We need you strong if we're going to keep going." And much as it galled Auric to admit, Teivel was proving to be a boon to their search party, even if they came up empty-handed again and again. But if it weren't for the vampire and his fighting skills, even Auric wasn't so arrogant to realize they would have long since perished.

They needed Teivel, and he, in turn, needed to eat.

At least the vamp realized it, too, and didn't argue any further. His fingers grasped Auric's arm and raised it to lip level. Auric turned his head, not wanting to watch, but he felt it, the sharp pinch of Teivel's fangs sinking into his flesh.

The pain proved fleeting, the tug on his arm strange, but it was the lassitude that entered his body and the pleasure that proved a surprise. Auric was a ladies man, and yet, the gentle tug of Teivel's mouth on his skin had his cock rising, hardening. It was embarrassing, and yet, he couldn't help the flush of heat.

Thankfully Teivel fed rapidly and released him with a nod of thanks. As soon as he stopped, Auric regained control of his body.

Nothing beat a moment to get renewed and refreshed, only a scant pause before they went off again, but this time, Auric watched the vamp's back, his expression thoughtful as he followed Teivel, who took point on their journey through the jungle.

While the thought of sharing Muriel with a third bothered the hell out of him, he couldn't deny Teivel did his damnedest to find her. The man had only shared a kiss with Muriel, a single embrace, and yet, he did not waver in his resolve to look. That kind of dedication earned him a grudging respect. It also made him realize that, as Nefertiti predicted, Muriel was drawing different brands of magic to herself.

But there was more to Teivel than the dark magic he might provide to Muriel. The man was a gifted fighter, but outside of battle he showed himself in possession of a dry humor that helped keep the situation from becoming too tense and fraught with despair.

Auric wasn't the only one to enjoy the other man's presence. He knew David had come to respect him over the course of the days and battles they'd spent together. Days ago he might have ranted and proclaimed the vampire would never lay a finger on Muriel, but now? Now he suspected, like it or not, the vampire might soon become a part of their growing family. If they ever found Muriel. That was looking more and more bleak, given they'd not found any traces of her presence since that first clearing. The closest they'd come was Azazel's stench, their only warning that more ambushes waited.

Auric took a break to drink some water—brackish crap he'd boiled from a tributary he'd found a day back. Teivel tapped his machete on his leg as he pivoted looking for the next clue.

Auric save me!

The frantic shout startled Auric, and he jumped, sloshing liquid down his sweat-soaked shirt. His eyes stared wildly about.

Teivel stood still, as if frozen. "Did you hear that as well?"

He'd not imagined it? Auric nodded.

David shifted from his panther. "I did, too. But where did it come from?"

Where indeed, because it certainly wasn't anywhere close in the forest. At the realization, Auric slumped and tapped his head. Somehow, Muriel had managed to send a mental call, and while it gladdened him to know she lived, it left them no closer to her than before.

"Call Gaia."

Auric lifted his head and peered at Teivel, wondering at his strange suggestion. "Why?"

"She might be able to portal us to where the

mental cry came from."

"Why not call Lucifer? Surely he can do it, too?"

Teivel grinned. "My Lord might be powerful, but truly, do you trust him to rummage through your mind to trace a mental call?"

The wince, while unbidden, proved the point. "Why can't you call Gaia?"

The big man rolled a shoulder. "I would, except evil, dead things with no souls don't exactly catch Mother Earth's attention."

Another good point. Feeling like an idiot, he called her name aloud. "Gaia." Nothing. He cleared his throat and called louder. "Gaia!"

A swirl of green formed by the edge of the woods, and from the mist stepped Gaia, crowned in a wreath of ivy and a diaphanous gown the color of springtime grass. "Have you found Muriel?" she immediately asked.

"Do you see her?" Auric retorted.

Gaia planted her hands on her hips. "Aren't you just a ray of sunshine? If you haven't found her, then why were you bellowing for me?"

David took a step forward. "We heard her. Muriel. In our minds." David tapped at his head. "We were hoping you could use her cry for help to pinpoint her location again and open a portal."

Gaia's gaze took in David's nude state in a slow up-and-down sweep that made him blush and drop his hands. "I must say, sometimes I do create the nicest things. As for finding her, hold my hands, and I'll see what I can do."

Auric didn't trust the sly look in her eyes, but they needed her help. He and David linked hands with her. Off to the side, Teivel watched with a cynical smile.

"Close your eyes," she ordered. "Now recall her words. Bring it to mind. Let me see it."

Auric recalled Muriel's panicked message. How it had appeared to come from afar, a single fragile link with his beloved, lost a moment later.

Gaia let out a noisy breath. "Well. Well. What do you know." She released their hands and took a step back.

"Do you know where she is?"

"I do."

"Take us there."

"I'm sorry, but I can't." Instead, she flung her hands toward them, propelling a powdery dust into their faces.

"You fucking bitch," was all Auric managed to mutter before he slumped to the ground next to an already unconscious David.

CHAPTER ELEVEN

*H*oly fuck!

I might have screamed it as I woke to pain, a ripping agony that made me scream. What was happening?

Opening my eyes proved a struggle, as they initially refused to cooperate. But I owned my body, and it would obey. I forced them open and had to blink, for surely I was caught in a nightmare. This couldn't be happening.

And yet it was.

A grotesque demon hunched over me, Azazel by the look of his black skin and large, curved horns. But it wasn't his appearance so much as his actions that concerned me. As I watched in horror, a keening sound whistled from my mouth as the bastard dragged a claw across my rounded abdomen, a diagonal slash that crossed over the first one.

X marks the spot was my hysterical, pain-riddled thought.

Using the tips of his claws, he pried at my flesh. A whimper escaped me as I fought against the nauseating pain.

"Careful you don't harm the babe."

The order distracted me, and my gaze left that of my massacred flesh to zero in on Lilith. I managed to gasp, "Bitch."

Lilith's piercing, raptor-like scrutiny focused on me. She smirked. "I prefer the term 'winner'. Now shut up as I prepare to greet my child."

I wanted to scream more invectives, and while I screamed as they parted the flesh of my womb, my return to cognizance ended up short-lived, as I passed out again.

The next time I regained consciousness, my whole midsection throbbed and a lassitude permeated my limbs. I looked for strength, anything to hold on to my thin thread of life, only to find nothing, as my magical reservoir bordered on empty. To my shame, I whimpered.

"What? Not dead yet? Aren't you just a stubborn one?" Lilith remarked.

My hands twitched, and I realized I'd been freed of my restraints. My hands slid down to cup my very flat abdomen covered in a sheet soaked in my own blood.

"My baby," I whispered.

"Right here," Lilith crowed triumphantly, waving a swaddled bundle in front of her.

"No." My refusal emerged weak, the fight in me drained along with my blood. "Why?" I rasped through lips dry and cracked.

"Why else but power? This little bundle of joy will aid me in taking my revenge on the world."

Her words took a moment to sink in, and when they did, tears seeped, hot as my shame over failing to protect my daughter. "But she's just a baby."

"How short-sighted, I see her more as a powerful tool." Lilith smiled, and the madness in it chilled me to the core.

"Let me see her," I begged.

I thought for sure she'd refuse, but to my surprise, Lilith lowered the bundle, and I saw her, my beautiful Lucinda. Her eyes were closed, her lips a perfect rosebud. Even though she'd grown so quickly, she was beautiful and healthy appearing, her cheeks round and flushed pink.

As if sensing my stare, she opened her eyes, and I

sucked in a tremulous breath at their vivid blue, which swirled into green with flecks of brown. A maelstrom of color representing all those who'd had a hand in creating her.

Lilith snatched back my baby girl, and I closed my eyes, not that it stopped the tears that leaked. "I hope you die a painful death."

The woman let out a witch-worthy cackle. "Not happening, not now that I have the baby. But you, on the other hand, won't prove so lucky. I've arranged something special for you. Azazel was most insistent he get to play with you, and since he proved a most handy helper, I see no reason why not."

I doubted Azazel would get the chance. I'd lost so much blood, and I could feel the chill creeping through me. It looked like I was not immortal after all. So much for good genes.

Blackness sucked at me, and filled with despair, I let it pull me in.

CHAPTER TWELVE

*W*ake.

The insistent message repeated over and over until, with a groan, Auric sat up.

What the hell? Why was he sleeping?

Gaia!

Memory of the betrayal wiped the last lingering traces of the sleep drug from his system. Auric rolled over and noted a still slumbering David in his cat shape. Before Auric could wake him, he released an agonized groan at what he saw beyond him.

"Muriel," he whispered. Not that his softly spoken word would wake her.

Lying still as a corpse, Muriel lay on the ground only a few feet from him, dressed only in a bloody sheet. Auric scrambled to her side and clasped her cold hand in his, the wail in him breaking free.

"No!" He screamed his denial to the sky, the world, to all who would listen.

"Holy fuck, are you trying to kill her with your goddamned caterwauling?"

Auric sucked in a breath and clenched his fists. "She's dead."

"Almost," Teivel announced, dropping to his knees on her other side. He placed his fingers on her neck. "Her pulse is weak, but she's still there."

Hope fluttered in his breast, and Auric took another look at her and, for confirmation, looked within himself. He found the connection that bound them together, soul to soul. She lived, if by a tendril. "I'll call Lucifer to heal her."

"No time," Teivel announced, taking out a sharp blade and slicing it across his wrist.

"What are you doing?"

"Giving her some blood. It's her only hope."

"How will that help her? She's dying, not thirsty."

"You call me the undead, and that is true, and yet, unlike zombies, vampires don't decay. The reason is this." Teivel held up a dripping wrist. "Our blood is what keeps our flesh from dying, and it can keep her from dying, too."

Auric wanted to protest. Giving her blood,

vampire blood, went against everything he'd been taught. And yet he couldn't let her die. "Do it."

"Thanks for your permission, your grace." Teivel shot him a sardonic smirk, as if to say there never was any doubt, and pressed his wrist to her lips.

Auric might have held his breath as he watched.

Muriel didn't move, not even to swallow. The vamp used his other hand to draw back the sheet, and Auric gasped in horror at the mess on her stomach. Someone had ripped her open, but for what purpose? Who would do such a thing?

Teivel dripped his blood over Muriel's wound, the dark drops spattering in a crimson shower and, more unbelievably, healing her. Before Auric's eyes, the skin pulled together, knitting itself in a macabre fashion he couldn't look away from.

Once again, Teivel pressed his wrist to Muriel's mouth, and this time, Auric saw movement. A reflexive swallow then another. Soon, she sucked at Teivel, but Auric didn't stop her. How could he when the bloom in her cheeks returned?

A growl let him know David was awake, and pissed. Was that why Teivel pulled his arm away abruptly? Muriel mewled in loss.

"What are you doing? She's not completely healed."

"There's no more time." Teivel peered into the shadows of the jungle around them. "The blood is drawing more monsters. Too many of them for us to fight while protecting her. We must leave now. Call a portal. I can't. My power is bound to my blood, and I've given her too much."

David paced in front of them, snarling at the encroaching shadows. Auric scooped Muriel into his arms, wincing when her face contorted. Her wounds were not fully healed, but they'd run out of time.

He called forth a portal, one as close as possible to Lucifer's castle. He stepped through just in time. Monsters leapt from the jungle with slavering jaws, dark eyes, and hungry expressions. David and Teivel leapt through the portal, slashing at grasping claws, severing them even as they leapt through. Once they cleared the interdimensional rip, Auric slammed it shut, severing a leaping beast in half.

The corpse twitched on the ground, and Auric wasn't too proud to admit he was glad to leave that forsaken place.

He held Muriel cradled to his chest, trying to be as careful as possible not to jostle her as he strode to the castle. Teivel covered their rear while David bound ahead and yowled a warning.

A movement caught his eye, and Auric looked

down to see Muriel's lashes fluttering. She finally wrenched them open, and he saw the relief in her eyes when she perceived him. "Auric," she whispered. "You saved me."

Not soon enough, his shame reminded. Auric's jaw tightened. "I wish I could take the credit, but it wasn't me. We found you."

"The baby..." Muriel's eyes fluttered. "Where's the baby?"

"What?" He tried to make sense of her words.

"Did you save our daughter, too?"

At the blank look on his face, she let out a small wail and passed out again.

Just what the fuck happened to her? And what baby is she talking about?

CHAPTER THIRTEEN

I feared opening my eyes, even if the agonizing pain was gone. The last thing I recalled I'd hovered on the threshold of life, left for dead. I remembered Azazel leering at me, detailing what he intended to do to my body. But…Azazel had died or was severely injured. Or had I dreamed the staff of wood that emerged from his chest, staking him like a vampire? And then the smell of spring grass and sunshine.

Mother? Had she come to save me, or had my inner desire to have her care cause me to imagine she'd come to my rescue? My mind moved sluggishly, my memories covered in a haze that pushed at me to forget. Like that would happen.

Lilith. The whisper of her name in my mind reminded me of that foul bitch and of my grievous loss. My hands moved of their own accord to cup my flat stomach. I pressed down, hoping to feel that burgeoning hardness, that sign of life I'd begun to enjoy before the nightmare began.

My flesh sank without resistance. I tore the sheet from me and inspected my bare stomach, the large X, an angry red scar that would always remind me of my failure.

Tears leaked from the corners of my eyes, but before I could begin to wail, strong arms, familiar arms, came around me, holding me tight.

Auric. My angel. I hadn't died after all, even if a part me thought I deserved to. I clung to him, sobbing. Now that he was here, he'd help me make things right. *He'll find our baby.*

He crushed me to him tightly as he feathered kisses across the top of my head, murmuring sweet nothings.

"Muriel, I thought I'd never see you again. I failed you." The anguish in his tone made me cry harder.

How close I'd come to losing him, and he to losing me. We were so tightly bound, our love, our lives. I meant everything to him—the other half of his soul, his prize for choosing damnation. I feared to contemplate what would have happened had I failed to survive.

"I'm alive, Auric," I whispered back. "You saved me. But our baby—" I choked, and he went still. "She's gone, Auric. Lilith took our child."

Stillness entered him as Auric leaned back. His green eyes peered at me intently. "What are you talking about? What child? Who's Lilith?"

Cold dread gripped me. "You can't have forgotten." My voice faltered at the expression on his face. "How could you have forgotten I was pregnant? Don't you recall? It's one of the reasons I was so pissed at my mother, because she wanted our child."

"You don't know who your mother is. Nobody does."

My mouth opened into an 'O' of surprise. "Of course I know who she is. She interrupted our dinner with my father and told me I was pregnant."

Auric shook his head in denial. "You're not making any sense. Perhaps you need to rest."

A flurry of motion distracted me, and I saw David rush into the room, only to get hip checked by my father, who dove on me with suspiciously bright eyes.

"Muriel!" He clasped me to him tightly, and I hugged my father back. Daddy would fix things.

"You need to find Lucinda," I begged.

"Who's Lucinda?" he asked in a careful tone.

"My daughter, your granddaughter. Lilith took her, and I think my mother knows where she is."

Stillness reigned in the room, and my dad pulled away from me. Three pairs of eyes watched me, confusion apparent in their depths. A chill settled on me. "No," I whispered, then more loudly, "Not you, too. How can none of you remember?"

"You've been through a traumatizing event," Auric placated.

My despair sloughed away in the face of their amnesia. "Don't you fucking bullshit me. There is nothing wrong with my mind. It's you who need to get yours checked." I started yelling, angry they couldn't remember. "After everything I went through—"

A prick in my arm made me turn my head wildly to the side, where I caught Nefertiti withdrawing a syringe.

"No, don't put me to sleep. You have to listen to me. We have to save her..."

Even though I fought the pull of the drugs, they dragged me down. I lacked the strength and magic to fight it—for now.

"I'm sorry, baby. We'll make you better," I heard Auric murmur, his voice choked.

But he didn't understand. Nothing would be better until I ripped that bitch Lilith's head from her shoulders and took back what was mine.

CHAPTER FOURTEEN

"*M*ommy."

The childish voice and demand in the tone made me whirl. There she sat, high up on the branch of a tree, her bare feet dangling, her brown hair caught up in pigtails. But it wasn't her normal appearance that caught me or the fact that she looked just like me in miniature. Her eyes, they swirled like a wave-tossed ocean, green to blue, blue to green, with specks of brown.

"Who are you?" I asked the question, even as part of me dared hope. Older than expected with her toddler size, but not out of the realm of possibility given the many planes of existence.

The child giggled. "Oh, Mommy. You're so silly."

"Lucinda." I breathed her name, fearing to break the mirage.

My little girl beamed at me. "I miss you, Mommy," she announced, her exuberance paling for a moment. "And I miss my daddies."

"Tell me where you are. I'll come get you." I'd fight to get her back. No one would take me unaware again, even if I had to take fifty more lovers to power my magic.

"It's a secret." The little girl held her finger up to her lips and gave an exaggerated shhh.

"I miss you, baby girl," I whispered, the tears choking my throat.

One moment she sat in the tree, and the next, she hugged my legs. I dropped to my knees and held her toddler body against mine, tears brimming hotly on my lashes.

Lucinda pulled from my grasp and shot a nervous look over her shoulder. "She's coming."

"Who?" I asked.

She didn't answer. Instead, she threw her arms about my neck and plastered a wet kiss to my cheek before running off into the mists of my dream.

I woke with tears running down my cheeks, which I quickly wiped with resolve. My daughter lived, and I didn't care how many people didn't believe me. I was going to get her back, by myself if needed.

And Lucinda had given me a clue where to start.

Time to pay mommy dearest a visit. It was past time for Mother Earth to meet the mommy from Hell, and boy was I pissed.

First, though, I'd need to fill up my magic tank.

Some would ask how I could think of sex at a time like this. Easily, and for several reasons.

One, the parasite, known as my power, hungered for it, and back in the land of the conscious, I could feel it calling to my lovers, calling for the aid it needed to replenish itself. The energy it needed for me to cause the havoc I so adored.

And second, I needed sex. I needed the close contact with my lovers, the reaffirmation that I lived, that I could prevail and I wasn't alone.

Three, super sex magic had once broken the spell on my mind. Maybe it would break the lock on theirs, too.

My body called for my lovers. My magic whispered on currents of air for them to come to me.

Come. To. Me.

The door sprang open, and Auric stalked in, David on his heels. Before they could slam the door shut, a third entered, and my eyes widened to see the vampire who'd kissed me.

Auric whirled and gave the vamp a hard stare.

The fanged one shrugged. "The blood I gave her binds us. Her magic calls to me, and I must answer."

"What's he talking about?" What blood? I didn't recall swapping fluids with the vamp, our kiss not having progressed that far. Just what had occurred while I lay passed out?

David, who'd crawled onto the bed, stripping his shirt as he came, answered. "Teivel was with us when we went into the wilds looking for you. When you suddenly reappeared on the brink of death, he gave you his blood to keep you alive."

"You let him feed me vampire blood?" I might have squeaked it.

"We had no choice."

No, but they did owe me an explanation. I told my hungry magic to shut up for a second and, with crossed arms, demanded they tell me everything.

I listened as they recounted their journey into the dangerous jungles of Hell, the attacks, my sudden reappearance, and the way the vampire had saved my life—and bound us for as long as I lived.

It occurred to me to throw him out. I had my hands full with two lovers, but even if I ignored my hunger for the cold power he promised, I needed every advantage I could get to save my daughter. I wasn't above using him for my own purpose, even if

Auric got mad at me for it. The saying it was easier to ask for forgiveness than permission applied here. And I was really good at asking for forgiveness on my knees, with my cheeks hollowed.

"He stays," I announced, and while David took it with his usual grin and shrug, Auric's body bristled.

"Are you sure about this?" His green eyes were flat, his expression a blank canvas. I couldn't tell what he thought. A part of me didn't care.

I hated to hurt my love, the other half of my soul, but I wouldn't forsake the child born of that love. "I love you, Auric. Nothing will ever change that. After all, I managed to find a way to love David without diminishing what I have with you. I don't love Teivel, which isn't to say I might not eventually, but I need what he can give my magic."

Auric's expression darkened. "You still think the hallucination about the baby is real."

"I don't think, I know. And once I'm all charged up, I'll prove it to you." I spoke with confidence, even if I didn't know how I'd accomplish it.

Teivel's triumphant smirk aimed at Auric annoyed me. The fact that I needed him didn't give him the right to slight my consort and first love. "You can stay, but no touching me. You haven't earned that privilege yet." That wiped his grin. I just hoped

I could hold true to my word, given my parasite seethed inside me, eager to replenish itself.

I beckoned Auric to me, letting the sheet fall. He fought it, not wanting to give in. But my magic wasn't pulling any punches. I hungered.

I leaned back as David plucked at one of my offered nipples, his latching mouth making me arch with a sigh of pleasure. "I need you, Auric," I whispered.

A second mouth attached itself onto my other pebbled berry, and I moaned. Auric hadn't been able to resist, thank Hell. I needed him. I twined my fingers into their hair and held them to me, my body already coming alive under their expert touch.

My eyes caught those of the vampire, and I licked my lips. Despite my demand he not touch, I couldn't deny his allure, his dark sensuality, which called to me.

Strip. I didn't speak the word aloud, but as if he heard my mental command, his fingers went to the buttons of his shirt. He peeled it from his torso, revealing a lean, muscled chest of alabaster. His jeans hung low on his hips, the vee of his muscles dipping below the waistband. *More. Show me more.* His eyes glinted with mischief as he obeyed, his hands drifting to his jeans and unbuttoning them in a slow reveal that transfixed me. My lovers, sensing my distraction, bit my nubs, making me cry out and flooding my pussy with wet heat.

Their coiling sexual excitement began to feed my starved power, each stroke of their tongues, each caress of their hands, making me stronger. More alive. The moisture in my cleft demanded penetration. That sensual fulfillment that only came with a cock.

Sucking in the sexual energy, I used it to brush David off and flip Auric onto his back. I straddled him, my sex hovering over his cock, my fingers digging into his pecs.

I impaled myself on his length, loving the way he arched up into me, stretching me. I rode my fallen angel, my channel sucking wetly at his rod, grinding myself against him. David helped me with my movement as the pleasure, in turn, rode me. He guided my motions with his hands on my hips, his cock pressing against my back, but allowing me my moment with Auric to reconnect, knowing his turn would come. I gyrated faster, our long absence from each other making us frantic. I came with a scream, my sex clamping in wild waves on his cock. Auric bellowed my name as he came, and the power filled me in an ecstatic rush.

I funneled that power right back at Auric, directing it. I caught his green gaze with mine, holding it. "Remember," I whispered. Then I slapped his mind with my esoteric force.

His back arched, and his face contorted as my magic burned the blocks in his brain, releasing what he had forgotten. I could tell the moment he recalled it all because his eyes filled with tears.

But he wasn't the only one who needed to remember. I rolled onto my back and beckoned at David, who was only too eager to obey. He caught my legs up and hung them over his shoulders, spreading me wide before plowing me with his length. My quivering channel took his hard thrusts, and begged for more. My reserves, depleted in my expenditure with Auric, sucked in this new source of sexual excitement. Faster and faster, David pummeled me, and when his thumb found my clit, the extra sensation sent me screaming over the edge again. I shook with the force of my orgasm, and David shuddered as I dragged him along with me for the ride. His ejaculation and bliss filled up my magical tank once again, and brimming to the rim with power, I forced it into his mind. I made him remember everything, and the shock of it made him roar.

He bounded off the bed, his reaction angry and animalistic in contrast to Auric's deep sorrow.

Sated, if somewhat depleted again, I couldn't help looking for the vampire. His dark eyes had bled to black as he watched our antics, and he stroked his cock. I rose from the bed and walked to him with undulating hips. My magic drove at this point, not done with its task. I stepped in front of the vamp, but when he would have touched me, I shook my head. His blood might have bound him to me, but it also gave me insight. I understood Teivel, understood what he wanted. See, while on the outside he projected a dominant and cocky persona, inside, what he truly craved was to belong—and to be owned by me.

"Hands behind your back and don't move."

His black eyes glowed with a frightful hunger that drew, rather than repelled, me.

I dragged a fingernail down his chest, and he shuddered. I circled my fingertip around his groin, avoiding his jutting cock. His breathing sped up.

A body brushed up against my back, and I leaned back into Auric's solid strength. He slid his hands around my body, briefly cupping my belly before sliding up to hold my breasts, his thumbs brushing my nipples.

"You owe him for saving your life," Auric murmured against my ear, making me shiver.

"And your jealousy?" I queried, knowing Teivel listened as we discussed his fate in our group.

"My love for you is stronger," was Auric's reply. Permission from Auric. And what about David? As if sensing my need of him, David appeared to stand behind Teivel. He didn't touch him, but I could see by Teivel's posture what it cost him to have another behind him, someone at his back. The fear to trust and, at the same time, the desire to trust. A yearning to no longer walk alone.

"We need him," David answered softly. "And he needs us."

This strangely emotional moment seemed almost surreal. Gone was the humor, the yelling and high-strung emotions that usually marked my decisions, but for something this important, the decision to invite a fourth into our happy menagerie could not be undertaken lightly, no matter the blood that bound me to him, no matter what my magic screamed.

Auric's hand caught mine and led it to Teivel's cock. "Touch him and make us all stronger. Give us what we need to fight."

You had to love my life. Permission to add another man to my bed? Only in my twisted world.

I clamped my hand tight around the vamp's cock, his flesh not cool like legend stated but hot, infernally so. I fisted him, grinning with satisfaction when he lost his cool and threw his head back with a moan.

Somehow, we ended up back at the bed with David sitting on its edge, his hard cock primed and ready. He lay back and Auric lifted me to sit on his cock, facing outward. I used my hands to brace myself on David's thighs as his hard length filled me. But the fun didn't stop there.

"Lean back," Auric commanded me, his eyes stormy with passion. I wondered at this new position and game, but did as told. I moved my hands to brace them on either side of David's torso, the front of my mound spreading and exposing itself. My new position also clearly showed the cock impaling me.

Teivel watched the erotic positioning as his eyes bled dark, his rod jutting from his body. His wasn't the only hard cock. Auric's long shaft had recuperated nicely from round one and made me salivate when I saw the pearly bead at its tip.

"Lick her." Auric spoke the order softly. I expected Teivel to protest, given my exposed pussy was currently intimately joined with David's prick, but without a cocky rejoinder, he eagerly bent to the task, his tongue darting out to flick against my clit. I groaned, and the muscles of my channel tightened, making David gasp.

"Use your tongue on her and make her hot," Auric murmured.

The more Auric spoke, the quicker and more elaborately Teivel plied his tongue, licking and nibbling my clit. I wondered if David was benefitting from some of the oral attention, too, for he growled and moaned under me, his hips bunching and thrusting as well as he could in our awkward position. As for me? I floated on a blissful cloud, the oral attention, along with the hard cock inside me, firing my desire.

"Turn her around." Auric controlled the action still, and with the help of several pairs of hands, they twirled me on David's cock until I faced him.

A callused hand I recognized as Auric's pushed me forward, exposing my ass to the men behind me. I didn't mind. I kissed David, the hot sweep of his tongue in my mouth making me sigh in pleasure.

Another tongue probed my bottom end, circling around my rosette, moistening it. Knowing what to expect, I relaxed and pushed out when a finger probed my tight ring, followed by a second, stretching and prepping me for more fun.

My kiss with David ended up broken off as Auric pulled me back upright so he could straddle David's chest, standing in a partial crouch that put his length level with my lips. He grabbed me by the hair—he knew how I liked it rough—and shoved his thick cock between my lips. I inhaled him deep, hollowing my cheeks as I sucked him hard, tasting his pre-cum on my tongue and loving it. Auric grunted as I grazed my teeth along his length.

I moaned around the rod in my mouth as I felt the third and final cock in the room probe my ass. I welcomed that hard length into my rosette with a keening cry. Then I lost my mind.

How could I not? They fucked me, all three of them at once in an indescribable orgy of pleasure. In my mouth gagging me, in my ass and pussy filling me. They thrust in and out of me in a synchronized cadence that made me orgasm hard, again and again. And still they plowed me. Their hands roamed all over my body, holding me, stroking me, pushing and pulling. They abused my flesh delightfully, and my magical beast sucked it up. And overflowed.

When my lovers came in an explosion that filled me with a bright white heat of ecstasy, I burned with the power of it. Glowed with the strength of it. It was too much, a sensual overload that required dumping. So I pushed the magic that spilled into me, pushed it outward in a shockwave that kept expanding as my lovers pulsed their releases inside me with cries of pleasure and tense bodies.

I don't know how long we remained in our rigid magical state. I do know I panted for breath when I finally remembered to take one, the surplus of magic thrust away from me, leaving me still full and satisfied.

I vaguely wondered what my wild power, carelessly flung, had done, but that required me to give a damn—something my closing eyelids and tired brain couldn't be bothered with. I fell asleep in a tangle of naked limbs. But not for long. Someone with no boundaries came barging in.

CHAPTER FIFTEEN

"*M*uriel!"

My father shouted my name from insanely close by jolting me from a sound—also known as a stupendous sex stupor—sleep. I only belatedly realized my nude state, and the fact that I was surrounded by naked male bodies. Ooh, so that orgy was not a dream. How wicked.

I'd have to explore my newfound status later though. Right now, I had a simmering father with crossed arms scowling at me, demanding my attention. I snatched at the blanket and covered my bosom before returning my father's glare. "Seriously, Dad, would it have killed you to knock?" It wasn't embarrassment that made me angry, more the fact that he'd ruined what I bet would have been some great morning nookie.

"My castle. My room. I can go wherever I want," he snapped.

"Fine. Then I guess we'll just leave." Two could play this game.

He narrowed his eyes at me. "You're testing my patience, Muriel."

"And you're getting on my last nerve," I retorted. "Now, care to tell me why your thong is in a knot?"

"Ha. I stopped wearing underwear a hundred years ago," my dad replied.

I screwed my face up. "Eew! Dad! That was a mental image I so did not need. Quick, say something else."

"Fine, I'll get back to the reason I'm here. You ruined one of my best hunters."

I peered over at Teivel, who watched the byplay with tousled hair and his lips half tilted into a smirk. I smiled back and winked at him salaciously. "Personally, I think I've improved him."

My dad growled. "How? By turning him into your own pussy-whipped bodyguard?"

"What can I say? I have talent." And speaking of whips, I wondered if my new sex slave would enjoy a beating administered by yours truly. I'd always found the concept of punishment intriguing.

"You're starting to take this sinning thing too far,"

Dad barked. "Enough already. You've proven you're my daughter with your countless sins and misdeeds. Don't you dare subvert any more of my key minions."

I grinned. "Why? You got anybody else I can use?"

My father harrumphed and changed the subject. "Anyway, that's not why I originally came to look for you. I don't know how you did it, but I remember everything, including your cow of a mother. I can't believe she managed to fuck my mind over like that a second time."

Neither could I, but that problem could wait for another day. I was fascinated to discover what my tidal wave of power had managed. Talk about awesome, if unintentional. "Dad, I hate to break it to you, but until you stop lusting after her, she's going to keep fucking with your mind. Or have you forgotten about a woman's greatest skill?" No one could quite figure out how it worked, but the fact remained, if a guy lusted after a woman, then she could screw with his mental state. In this case, wipe it clean.

My dad let out a string of curse words that made me giggle, but David blushed.

"Don't worry, Dad. No need for chemical castration, even if your plastic surgeons are probably drooling at the prospect of all the surgery." Those evil bastards. "I'm going to take care of Gaia," I announced grandly.

"Of course you are," my father replied with an evil twinkle in his eye. "Revenge, after all, is our middle name."

Actually mine was Muriel—I hated my first name of Satana—but I wouldn't split hairs. "Glad you're on board. Does that mean you'll help me with my plan?"

Auric groaned behind me. "Oh no, not another one of your plans. Don't listen to her, Lucifer."

I threw Auric a scowl. "My plan is good this time. I swear."

"Good like the morning you decided to surprise us with breakfast in bed?"

I managed not to redden at the reminder. "It was time you bought a new stove anyway."

"What about the time you got me a baby dragon for my birthday?"

I shrugged at my dad. "How was I to know its mother would come looking for it? Now stop harassing me and listen because, this time, it's a good one."

"What's good?" asked Bambi, walking in. She stopped dead. Her jaw dropped, and if her eyes opened any wider, they'd fall out. "Lamb! What the hell? Three men?"

I grinned sheepishly. "Would you believe it happened by accident?"

Bambi rolled her eyes. "Only with you." Her eyes then flitted from one naked man in my bed to another, rousing my newest green friend—jealousy. "My, your choice in flavors is varied," she purred.

"Down, succubus. You've got a man of your own."

That made her scowl. "Not exactly. He's been playing hard to get. But I have a plan to make him jealous with a guy I know who just came back from the war overseas, and might I add, it's been a while since he's had a woman."

"Soldier?" I queried.

"What and piss daddy off with a noble sort? Nah, he's a journalist."

"Good girl," my father praised her, and Bambi just about choked. Dad didn't often spread his love.

"But I have to say, I am envious. Three men. Yum." She licked her lips. "One more and you'll tie my record."

"Four men, eh?" I mused.

"Don't even think about it," Auric grumbled.

I laughed. With all my family rallying around

me, my confidence in my plan grew. "Hey, big sister, want to go on a rescue mission to save Lucinda?"

"Isn't she still like a tadpole in your belly?" Apparently someone needed to be brought up to speed, but once Bambi knew the score, she was determined to aid in the rescue. "What can I do to help get my niece back? The little hooker boots I bought her are nonreturnable, so we need to get moving before she outgrows them."

I elbowed Auric before he could say a thing, and at my pointed look, David elbowed Teivel for me. Bambi could dress my daughter any way she liked so long as underwear was worn and not optional.

"Why don't the boys and I get dressed then we'll meet you and Dad in the war room. Oh, and someone needs to get Nefertiti. We're going to need her help, too."

My dad stalked off, muttering something about his black cape, which had better be back from the cleaners, while Bambi winked at me and told me to enjoy my shower.

Boy, did I ever—on my knees, against the wall, and bent over. By the time we were done, not only was I squeaky clean everywhere I also fairly burst at the seams with magic.

Dressed and grinning like loons, my boys and I

went to the war room, where I outlined my plan, and to everyone's surprise, it was a good one. But I already knew that. It took us a few days, long impatient ones, to set our plan into motion. I used that time to help Nefertiti devise a spell to complete one phase of it—the part that would render Lilith impotent. What a shame my part of the plan required me elsewhere. I wouldn't have minded grabbing a bag of popcorn and watching how Nefertiti powered the spell with an orgy of a hundred and fifty men. Maybe she'd tape it and post it on HellTube.

The moment to act arrived, and everyone took their places as I prepared to enter Eden's garden alone.

Auric pulled me aside before my departure. "I don't like this part," Auric grumbled as he hugged me tightly.

I leaned my head against his chest. "I can do it."

"I know you can. I just wish you didn't have to do it alone."

I loved that he finally recognized my strength and loved him even more for worrying about me. "I love you." I stared up into his eyes. "You've put up with a lot, and I don't just mean the havoc that comes with my parentage. I know it hasn't been easy dealing with my magic and its needs. I don't know if I could be so understanding were the roles reversed."

"Well, I'm still not too crazy about the vampire. But I love you, and sharing you is a small price to pay to spend eternity with you. Now, go get our daughter back and know we won't be far. And if you're a good girl"—he dipped his head to brush his lips across mine, creating a sensual shiver in my body—"we'll tie you down and eat you until you scream 'more'."

Auric always did know just the right thing to say. David took his turn next hugging me and murmuring his love as he rubbed his cheek against mine in feline fashion. The vampire, now that we both stood dressed, just gave me a sardonic grin.

"I'd wish you luck, but you've already got all the horseshoes you need up your ass. So, instead, I'll say thanks for allowing me to join your circle."

"Ah, shut up." I yanked him to me and hugged him tightly. What could I say? The damned vamp was growing on me, and in spite of my doubts, my heart widened to include him.

"Are you done already? We are in Hell, after all, not some fucking hippy love fest," my dad interrupted, his disgust evident.

Just for that, I planted a noisy, wet kiss on his

cheek that had him harrumphing and turning shades of burgundy.

"Let's do this." Anticipation coursed through my body. I lived for danger and the thrill of the battle, and this definitely counted as a major one.

My dad sketched the portal to the Garden of Eden. He'd gotten the coordinates from his brother, God—they'd played cards for it. My dad, of course, cheated and won.

The swirling doorway appeared, and I prayed my theory was right as I entered it to confront my mother and Lilith. Two birds with one stone—or, in my case, two bitches with my boots up each of their asses.

One moment I stood in the ash-laced air of Hell, and the next, I stepped into a humid jungle, one not as neatly kept as the one I'd visited previously. The place seemed wilder while the sky's blue appeared off, not quite the beautiful clear color I remembered.

Lacking patience and subtlety, I got straight to the point and bellowed, "Mother!" I tapped a foot as I waited, and when she didn't immediately appear, I yelled again. "Gaia, you little bitch, get your mother-earth ass out here right now before I raze your precious Garden of Eden to the ground."

Apparently, in an effort to woo my mother, God

had given her the place as a courting gift. Being a selfish cow, she'd taken it, but never put out in return. As for my dad's method to get in her pants? He'd called her an uptight bitch—the perfect come-on line to get a woman to spread her legs. Go figure.

Leaves rustled, and from the branches stepped Gaia, but not the calm, collected one who enjoyed pissing me off. Her face appeared drawn, and circles of fatigue outlined her eyes. A tangled mess of hair crowned her head from which poked twigs and leaves. Her gown bore ragged holes while her bare feet peeked from the hem, stained brown with dirt.

I whistled. "Jeez, Mom. Talk about letting yourself go. How are you supposed to win Dad back looking like a refugee?"

"Shh!" she hissed, her frightened eyes darting erratically to peer at the woods around us.

I arched a brow. "Excuse me, but you do not shh me. Not when you've got a ton of explaining to do, starting with, where the fuck is my daughter?"

"Please, you must leave before she finds us."

"Who? Lilith?" I bared my teeth in a feral grin. "But I want her to find me. She and I need to have a talk." My itchy fist and sharp-edged sword were impatiently waiting to get acquainted.

My mother straightened, and her face took on

the haughty expression I'd come to expect from her. "You're going to ruin everything."

"Really? Why not explain what you're doing and obviously failing at?"

Gaia's lips tightened.

I chuckled. "Oh really, you are so fucking transparent. I grew up with the king of lies and deceit. Let me tell you how I see it, and you can correct me if I'm wrong. After putting the boys to sleep in the jungle, defenseless"—I added pointedly with a glare—"you ported your ass over to Lilith's hideaway. Somehow, you managed to steal the baby from her and teleported my ass out of there, saving me from certain death, for which I'll give you grudging thanks. Then you expected to hide the baby in your garden and keep her to yourself after wiping everyone's mind of her and then, when she was old enough, using her to fight Lilith. How am I doing so far?"

"You weren't supposed to remember anything," she grumbled.

I snorted. "Fuck with my mind once, shame on me, twice and you're lucky I haven't killed you yet. Anyway, as I was saying, you obviously didn't count on Lilith following you back to your precious garden."

"She was supposed to be banished for life." Gaia's disgruntlement over that error almost made me laugh.

"In case you hadn't noticed, Lilith's been practicing all kinds of evil magic. Did you think your little magical fence would stop her? It didn't impede me."

"So I noticed," Gaia remarked dryly.

I stuck my tongue out at her. Things were about to get resolved, my way, because, after all, the world, Hell, and, now, even Eden, would revolve around me and my needs. "So how long did you figure you could play hide and seek from Lilith before she caught you and Lucinda?"

"You think you know everything, don't you?"

I pretended to think about that, tapping my chin. "Actually, I know everything I need to. And I know your plan sucks."

"But—"

I narrowed my gaze and lost my jovial attitude. "Listen up, bitch. Because of you and your machinations, Lilith almost got her hands on my daughter. Lucky for you, I survived both your stupid games. Now, hand my daughter over, or I'll take your precious garden apart leaf by fucking leaf until I find her."

I could feel my gaze heating up, and judging by the way my mother stepped back, I guess the flames of Hell were dancing brightly in my eyes. Now, if only I could turn on that neat trick during power failures, I'd never need candles again.

"But the destruction I saw in my vision—"

"Is going to happen in about three seconds if you don't give me my child!" I yelled, done with her stalling.

"You would destroy the world?" Gaia's eyes widened. "For the sake of one?"

"You messed with the wrong mother from Hell. No one takes my child. Now, what's it going to be?"

Gaia sighed, and her shoulders slumped. "Fine. Take her back. I hope you know what you're doing."

I didn't, but I also didn't care. Lucinda belonged with me and her fathers.

"Mommy."

The childish voice from behind me had me turning and opening my arms wide for the little body that hurtled toward me. I hugged Lucinda to me tightly and stood up, cradling her on my hip.

"You found me," she whispered as her chubby arms wound tight around my neck.

"Always," I replied in a voice tight with emotion. My daughter's eyes held knowledge far beyond the age of her tiny body. Lilith and my mother might have forced her to lose her baby years with their petty games, but I'd do my best to ensure she enjoyed the best childhood from this point forth. I turned back to face my mother, who shook her head sadly.

"Your greed to have your daughter with you will cost us the world. You've played right into Lilith's hands."

As if her words summoned her, the sky above us darkened. A roiling black cloud crept in, overpowering the blue sky. Lucinda popped a thumb into her mouth and tucked her head into my shoulder. I didn't detect fear in her, just curiosity as to what would happen next.

Stay tuned, as this mommy from Hell is about to kick some serious ass.

I waited with more patience than I felt for Lilith to make her grand entrance, and when she did, to the flare of lightning and roll of thunder, I yawned. "Boring. Don't you know pyrotechnics are so eighties."

Still dressed in a boring robe, Lilith faced me, her tight lips flattened into an almost invisible line. "What a shame you survived. I'll have to rectify that, right after you hand over the child."

A taunting smile pulled the corners of my mouth. "Is this where I say, 'over my dead body'?

How cliché. There is only one possible outcome here, and it involves a lot of screaming, mostly by me, as I cheer on your demise."

I swear my taunts almost made her head explode. Her face turned a mottled red, her fists clenched so tightly I expected to see blood dripping, and she came close to spewing smoke from her ears.

"Laugh all you want, you spawn of the devil. I will prevail. You can't hope to beat me in a contest of power."

My lessons on smirking, taught by my dad, meant I gave her the whopper of all smirks. "I thought pissing contests were reserved for men. Seriously. You chose the wrong princess to mess with. I'll give you one last warning to back off and forget about touching my daughter." I lied of course. Lilith wouldn't leave this garden alive. Besides, I didn't figure she'd agree.

"So be it," she intoned.

I sensed movement behind me as Lilith played her treacherous hand. I whirled, the words to a spell on the tip of my tongue, ready to blast Azazel as he dropped down from the trees to attack me. Apparently, my vague recollection of his death wasn't quite true. No problem. I'd resolve that in a moment.

With a scream, Gaia threw herself in front of

him, protecting me with her body. Stupid bitch—I had this fight. His claws, meant for me, entered her stomach and exited her back, dripping in green ichor. Gaia slumped to the ground.

"Mom?" I stared in disbelief as the woman I'd scorned gave her life for me, uselessly, as I'd expected this attack and would have easily repelled it.

"I'm sorry." My mother's whispered words hurt me, but not as much as I'd hurt Azazel for taking her from me.

Even that revenge became lost to me. The earth under my mother's body heaved, and from the ground where her blood soaked it, sprang roots, gnarly living things that flailed in a macabre dance. They whipped around my mother's body and dragged her back into the ground. But that was not all they did.

They wrapped around Azazel, and though the demon slashed and pulled, the roots twined about him, dozens, hundreds, until all that remained were his eyes. I quite enjoyed their wide, wild look, the dawning horror. Cocooned, the earth opened up and swallowed Azazel whole.

It seemed killing Mother Earth had pissed off the garden. That, or demons made great fertilizer. Either way, that treacherous villain was gone.

Which left only one threat.

I whirled back to Lilith in time to catch her raising her hands and chanting words of power. The magic in the air gathered, electrical zings that made my hair stand on end. Probably not a good sign. But again, my plan had predicted this.

"Ready, baby girl?" I whispered to my daughter. Lucinda gave a slight nod. Linked by proximity, I drew on my daughter's untutored power as Nefertiti had taught me. Alone, I lacked the strength, but together, with my little atom bomb, just call us unstoppable.

Lilith stalked toward me, lightning dancing from her fingertips, her expression as dark as the storm she'd called. I felt the slam against my mental shields first. However, I'd learned a lot since Gabriel had played with my mind. I giggled at her attempt. "Ooh, that tickles. Do it again." Unlike before, not only did I have my own power times three I also drew on Lucinda's raw magic as well and rebuffed the mental invasion without breaking a sweat.

Lilith snarled. The ground under my feet rumbled, and the crashing sound of toppling trees echoed. Cracks zigzagged toward me, threatening to swallow me whole. So I floated above the heaving earth and drove Lilith even crazier.

Rule number one when in a fight—never lose your temper. Rule number two—be sure to provoke that of your opponents. And rule number three—cut them off from their source of power. Lilith's strength, while formidable on its own, required the consumption of souls stolen from Hell for truly remarkable heights. Naughty me, I'd cut her off from her magical battery.

See, I'd predicted Lilith would go after the damned ones to fuel her attack. Too bad it wouldn't work. Nefertiti, enjoying herself in a Guinness-record orgy, had locked those souls down tight with the erection—pun intended—of a shield around Hell. No access to the damned souls meant no more magic for Lilith.

Boo-fucking-hoo.

With a serene smile to rival a certain famous painting, I watched as Lilith threw magical attacks at me: lightning, fire, wind, more mind invasions. Her power waned, and I watched as she tried to draw on her previous fount of souls and came up dry.

"What have you done?" she screeched.

I batted my lashes innocently. "Who me?" Lucinda giggled at my exaggerated tone, a sweet sound that spurred me to end this, once and for all.

"I don't need magic to kill you," she spat, stalking closer to me.

"But you could have used friends."

"Who says I didn't bring any?" She let out a sharp whistle.

I snickered, truly enjoying myself and without having shed any blood—yet. "Oops, did I forget to mention I brought some of mine along to play with yours? Oh, boys," I sang.

They strode from the woods of Eden, my trio of men dressed in black leather and looking wickedly delicious. With them came my dad, dressed in his black cape and looking suavely dangerous. My father threw a decapitated demon head at my feet.

"Happy birthday," Daddy declared.

"I still want a cake," I announced. "A pink one," I added, just to get that pained look on my dad's face.

"I'll take her now," said Bambi's soft voice from behind me.

I hated to give Lucinda up, even for a short moment, but I didn't want her to see what came next. I wanted the first time she saw blood to be like other girls, when she was a teenager at school in white pants getting her period for the first time.

"Go with your Aunt Bambi while Mommy takes care of this."

"Wuv you, Mommy."

Yeah, for those words, I'd lay waste to the worlds. And for the sloppy kiss I got on the cheek, I'd give her the universe.

Lucinda held out her arms and went to my sister, who drew a portal and took her back to my dad's castle.

Little one out of the way, I prepared to get even. "Prepare to meet justice, my justice," I told Lilith with a smile that tended to send those with a healthy respect for living running.

Lilith stamped her foot. "This isn't over. You might capture me now, but I'll escape your father's Hell just like I escaped Limbo, and when I do, you'll pay."

"Yeah, about that whole eternal damnation and torture thing. See, I have this policy of not leaving loose ends. So kiss your life goodbye." I stalked toward Lilith, pulling my Hell blade free as I strode, its gleaming red blade shining eagerly for the violence I would unleash.

That wiped away her smile, for about a second. Then it returned. "I'm immortal. You can't kill me. No matter what you do, I'll—"

I begged to differ. I swung my sword and sent her head flying. My men then joined me in dismembering the scorned bitch, and then my dad called portals to all the planes he knew. All of us took a piece and walked through a portal, returning only after burying our piece nice and deep. See, the thing about immortality was, yes, the flesh lived forever, but cut it into enough pieces and death suddenly didn't look so bad.

Eden itself took care of Lilith's head as if catching on to my plan, sucking it down into its earthy depths, where I hoped the worms would eat her eyeballs.

"I can't believe that worked," Auric said, shaking his head.

"That was barely a fight," grumbled my father, who looked splendid in his Darth Vader cape and boots.

David, looking sexy in leather, just grinned while Teivel rolled his eyes. "And I thought I was a whack job. You guys are fucked."

"Welcome to the family," I said with a bright smile. My family. And it now had a motto, *Touch them and die.* I wondered how it would look embroidered in Latin.

*W*eeks later...

I LOUNGED on our new back patio overlooking my new oversized yard, more of a field really, only the best for his girls, or so my dad claimed when he helped me buy the property. Independence was all well and good, but with a kid, three lovers, and my fetish for shoes, I needed the space. Never fear, though, while daddy dear had bought the place, he'd not required me to sign anything.

The shock just about killed me, and I could tell it hurt him, too. Generosity wasn't in his nature, but as he confided to me when he handed over the keys,

"Knowing your men are living in the house I bought them is payment enough."

The funny thing was, while the old Auric might have let pride stand in the way of the awesome mansion, the angel who'd almost lost it all had learned to live with some things, such as a kick-ass alarm system, replete with motion detectors and cameras, plus an esoteric shield to prevent things from portaling in.

Except for Dad of course. Nothing could keep him out.

Nothing could also keep him away. Daddy dear wasn't the only one fascinated by Lucinda. The child was perfect. The world might revolve around me, but the sun, the moon, my life revolved around her.

She fascinated me, even as she did the simple things, like now for instance. I watched with more contentment than I'd ever thought possible as Lucinda played with her new hellhound puppy. She'd named the muscled critter with glowing red eyes Fluffy. I thought my dad would have a stroke when he heard.

After the initial scramble to find a bigger house, dress my little girl in all things pink and frilly, and make sure the bar had survived during my absence, this was the first day I'd had in what seemed like ages to relax.

I'd expected motherhood to shock my system and turn my life upside down, and while it had in a sense, I was the first to admit I loved it. As did my men. Auric and David made perfect fathers, not that I'd had any doubt. Lucinda, true to her genes, had them wrapped around her little finger. Given her daddies' protective instincts, I couldn't wait until she started dating. Auric would have a cow, and David would probably eat the unlucky boy.

Speaking of whom, from the bushes slinked a blond panther, low to the ground and silent. Lucinda, though, always knew when he got close, a trick I wouldn't have minded. She whirled around screaming like a banshee before she pounced on David. The two rolled in the grass, just another normal little girl and her oversized cat. How domestic.

A puff of brimstone mixed with sunshine let me know Mom and Dad had arrived. My mother's demise had been premature—how unfortunate. Apparently, the earth had swallowed her in order to protect and heal her. Must have been some pretty good freaking dirt because the Gaia that emerged wasn't quite the bitch I recalled. For one, she called me regularly to chitchat, of all things, and even threatened to come for tea. She also appeared to be attempting to patch things up with my dad, which really grossed me out, especially when my dad winked at me and said maybe they'd try for baby number two.

My dad gave me a punch in the shoulder as he walked past, his new version of public affection, which beat the previous of none at all. My mother sat beside me, and together we watched as my dad pulled his exorcist routine for his granddaughter. Lucinda clapped her hands and giggled then squealed, "Again."

Auric came from the house and groaned. "Please tell me your dad's not spinning his head again."

I just grinned in reply. If he thought that was bad, just wait until he found out about the dragon my dad had given her.

Auric manhandled me onto his lap, and I snuggled into his arms. My life couldn't get any more complete, from the vampire sleeping in my basement, who had wormed his way into my heart, to the giant kitty on my lawn, whom I adored, to my fallen angel, who kept proving his love to me. Who said a princess of Hell couldn't have it all?

As for the future and the calamities it probably

held in store for me? Bring it. I feared nothing, not with my family—strange as it was, with my dad currently blowing flames from his nose—by my side. This princess of Hell had faced off against evil and adversity, and guess what? I'd won. My prize? A whole lot of freaking love—and sex. Sweaty, screaming, thigh-clenching sex. Oh my.

A breeze lifted my hair, the smell of it oddly reminding me of the sea. Impossible, given there wasn't a body of water anywhere close by. For a moment, I thought I could hear the crashing of waves, taste the brine of the ocean on my tongue, a watery caress.

I wondered what the family would think of a vacation at the beach.

***Find out what happens next in* <u>Vacation</u>**
<u>**Hell,**</u> where Muriel, instead of collecting seashells like a normal person, picks up a new man. A merman...